Also by Christian Hendrix:

A (Prom)ise

A Need For Charlie

The Roaches of Grove

You Can't Go Home Again

By Christian Hendrix

GRASS VALLEY PUBLISHERS
SAINT PAUL
LLC

Library of Congress Cataloging-in-Publication Data
Names: Hendrix, Christian, author
Title: You Can't Go Home Again / Christian Hendrix
Description: First edition. | Saint Paul : Grass Valley Publishers LLC, [2024]
Identifiers: Library of Congress Control Number: 2024905812 (print) | ISBN: 9798990225305 (print) | ISBN: 9798990225312 (ebook)
Subjects: LCSH Young women--Fiction | Homecoming--Fiction | Female friendship--Fiction | Fathers and daughters--Fiction | Sisters--Fiction | Cults--Fiction | Terrorism--Fiction | Two thousands (Decade)--Fiction | California--Fiction. | LCGFT Bildungsromans | Alternative histories (Fiction) | BISAC FICTION/GENERAL | FICTION/ALTERNATIVE HISTORY | FICTION/LITERARY | FICTION/THRILLERS/TERRORISM | FICTION/WOMEN

Written by Christian Hendrix
(christian.hendrix.47@gmail.com)

Cover illustration by: Deborah Frost
Back cover photo: Courtesy of Guillaume Issaly under the Unsplash license

Contents

Part 1
Love Bomb

So where are you?

Besides this large, ridiculous tin box, crammed with dim souls. Why are you the only light in this excessive and unnecessary wind tunnel? The afternoon is late and the colors are fading. They talk to and comfort you, they whisper that everything will be okay-- as long as you remember what they said.

The chalky, gray November skies remind you of a world you used to glimpse, one that was never that far away, but always behind and beneath you. Will you have the light to resist that world's charms? Will you be able to make peace with your past so that you may focus on your future?

Your stomach writhes in knots trying to come up a with correct answer. *Any* answer. You remember the light you are filled with, and the light that will soon be spread, and your skin stops crawling. Your brothers and sisters await you in Makaan. They are waiting behind you, for you are the brave conquistador of centuries past that paves the way for a clear and autonomous future. One not made of cheap rhetoric and hate below the surface of its meaning, but one made of new beginnings, new meanings and a new dawn.

The light of your current world continues to fade like the light of the past. One of the blind entities asks you if you require more resources, for that is what it is all about: excess, indulgence. You smile the only smile you ever knew, the one that prepared you for Isik. The one that will get you through this dark tunnel when your transfer lands and your feet are back on the muddy ground of this hopeless beyond.

You think about the duties you've been assigned, but not the rewards you will reap. You think of your brothers and

[6]

sisters behind you, and the ones thereafter that will follow your contribution. You used to wonder about the world, but now you have seen a great deal of it. You have found what you were looking for. You are where you belong, able to hide in plain sight without letting your dignity ruin you like so many others let theirs' ruin them.

Your sense of pride brims with the light you carry within you. There is no pain or death or darkness, you have no more need for them. You can only cry tears for the life you once had, but not the life you let go. They are not the same, they told you it could never be. Your work can not be undone even if you yourself tried to undo it.

The hard part's over, all that's left, is the waiting. And of course, the goodbye.

"She's heeeere!" Scarlett screamed from up the driveway. The other three girls ran giddily down the walk to greet her where the taxi pulled up to the gate.

All Vincent Adams could do was beam a relieved sort of smile that told him his daughter had landed safely after flying high for so many years. He couldn't even recognize the tension that had been slowly building ever since the last time he saw her. He only saw it replaced with another kind as she stepped out of the taxi.

Lenoir had been an enigma wrapped in a riddle for most of her young life. Her recent choices had been particularly perplexing to him. Just why did she have to go traipsing all around the world for so long? Why did she refuse his invitation—no – his request to pick her up personally from the airport? And why did she not come home straight away after September 11th? Indeed, what an uncertain world it has become. Since the attacks in New York, it felt like a new kind of world, and for the first time since she was six and wandered into a hornet's nest and suffered an allergic reaction, Vincent Adams was petrified of the world his daughter would inherit.

But all that worrying, all that planning for her future, and his; as uncertain as they both seemed, it would come later. After all, she was home now. That was what mattered. The prodigal daughter had returned, what else did he need?

She came into view as he dug out his wallet to pay the cab driver. Her friends were jumping up and down and squealing in a language that was foreign to Vincent. It only consisted of a random series of high-pitched giggles and frittered words that only came out in torrents. He was torn between greeting his daughter and paying off the cabbie, but once Piper and Ramona got all three of her small bags out of the backseat, the decision was made.

Vincent circled around the taxi with three bills poking out of his fist just as Lenoir caught sight of him.

[8]

"Wait," her voice was firm, yet soft.

"Hey kid," he grinned.

"What are you doing?" she smiled back in an unusual way.

"I was going to pay the man for services rendered," he turned the bills out.

"I got this dad," she brought out a wallet with a ray of light stitched on it. He suspected it was constructed of hemp.

"Oh okay," he raised his hands in the air, feigning surprise. But he wasn't surprised at all. She had been doing this sort of thing all her willful life. Her friends looked on with mild amusement as well, knowing full well that the same old Lenoir had come back to them. Vincent was always happy to be able to provide for his daughter, but with her convictions, her independent spirit, her stubbornness, it wasn't always the easiest race to win.

As she rifled through the coins and bills she had accumulated throughout her travels, Vincent thought about her sixteenth birthday when he had bought her a decent used car. She stood there with her hand upon her hip like her mother used to, in front of all her friends, not malicious or sarcastic like most teenagers, not embarrassed, just matter of fact when she addressed him about why she couldn't accept his generous gift. A few months later, she had saved up enough money to buy herself a clunker of a Toyota that served her well enough until the end of high school.

Once the cabbie was paid and gone, the six of them stood awkwardly at the end of the driveway, watching her with fresh eyes.

Vincent approached and took his little girl in his arms. Not since the hot desert airstrip in Pakistan had they last embraced, and even though it had been a little more than a year ago, it might as well have been a century. "You feel frail," he noted, "have you eaten yet?"

"I had some corn nuts at the terminal in Tokyo," she smiled warmly. "I had forgotten how much I love corn nuts." Piper made a sarcastic face, "Eww, it's all about Doritos."

Lenoir approached her sister next, "Yeah, I forgot about Doritos too!" She hugged her serenely.

Piper looked confused at the soft and slow way her elder sister took hold of her.

"I could run to the store," Vincent offered. "I'm afraid things have been a little crazy around here."

"Is that why we've been ordering Indian every night?" Piper droned.

"So, are you tired?" Alice asked. "How long have you been travelling?"

"Wow, I don't even know," her eyes cast up, admiring something. A late fall breeze blew through their quiet neighborhood. A few scraps from the nearest loose leafed bushel embedded themselves in her hair which had lightened considerably out there in the desert sun. She shook her head, causing them to float away. "I don't even think I could tell you what day it is. So many time zones," she laughed nervously.

"Did you sleep at all on your flights?" Alice pressed, a rare occurrence.

"I guess I probably did. Mostly I read. I just did a lot of soul searching. It feels so strange to be back here. It's like going back to a previous life after living something completely different for so long."

Her friends watched her with amazement. The spiraling butterfly in Vincent's stomach didn't let up. He was so happy to see his daughter, but something persisted in his conscience. It was some kind of dread. He wasn't sure why. He had been absolutely giddy when Lenoir phoned last week announcing her return. Now that she was here, safe but tired from travelling, *now* he worried about her. As if a few days at home wouldn't bring her bubbly self back to the surface.

[10]

It was indeed strange. While she was gone, he hardly thought about it, except when he heard about the attacks. And remembering his lack of concern only brought out more flashes of dread. Did that make him a bad parent? Of course, he could cite the usual excuses; his company taking off, endless hours working both at the office and home. Bringing up Piper, who proved to be less independent and a completely different kind of concern than Lenoir was at her age. But Vincent had to remind himself that all these feelings were temporary and that they all had some adjusting to do to her being back. Four years is a long time, he reminded himself.

"Well, you have to start talking. Tell us a couple of stories to tide us over," Ramona chided.

Lenoir smiled, "I was thinking how I was going to go about doing that on the planes."

"While you are sorting that out, why don't we go up to the house and have some iced tea? How does that sound girls? I found your favorite a while ago and bought it on a whim before I even knew you were coming back. The kind you used to always drink, unsweetened Javanese. How does that sound?"

She smiled quietly again, "Sounds like a dream, dad." As they drank tea and lounged in the sunroom overlooking the valley below, Lenoir told them a story from her first year. It was about how a British couple, also travelling in Turkey at the time, had taken her under their wing, and that she had stayed with them because she was homesick for any kind of English conversation. Eventually the couple had begun to fight about trivial things and the wife took her aside one morning while they were touring an ancient city, begging Lenoir to take her with her wherever she was going. That she was willing to leave her husband to become her full-time travel companion.

"Travelling companion?" Ramona snorted. "Did she have a thing for you?"

[11]

"No," Lenoir laughed meekly, "what she actually said was 'chaperone'. She wanted to mommy me. If you had met this woman, she was a total caretaker and her husband was completely dependent on her. I expect they were back together again by the time it was time to go home to Birmingham. Oh boy, they were so dysfunctional. I just had to ditch them."

"How'd you do it?" Scarlett asked.

"I convinced them to take a train to Erzurum, which was the direction I was heading anyway, but I snuck out at Erzincan while they were bickering about who should go get breakfast at the food car. At that point, I just wanted to be on my own again. It was the experience that taught me to fully immerse myself in my surroundings. I had pined for English and all things west but look what it got me."

They laughed politely at the moral of her tale, but the day was getting late and Lenoir was obviously exhausted, even if she insisted she wasn't.

After a moment of silence, she shook her head as if reminded of something, but remained soundless. Vincent watcher her acutely, unable to shake that draining feeling inside him that told him something was wrong.

But he was distracted by Scarlett crying out, "I can't believe it has been four years!" She sprung up from the couch next to Alice and attacked Lenoir where she sat in the wicker chair and viciously hugged her.

"Did you get my postcards?" Lenoir smiled deeply as she hugged her back.

"Of course I did!" Scarlett tittered. "I only wish I could have sent a few back your way."

"Yeah," Ramona folded her arms, "Why no return address?"

Lenoir shrugged, "I was always on the move. I didn't know where I would be from one day to the next."

"That is such a *you* thing to say," Ramona laughed.

"It's funny," she shook her head. "Everyone always makes

all these grand plans after high school. They're going to college, they're going backpacking through Europe, they're going to get married, their moving like an army of ants up one side of the world and down the other. You plant yourself right in the middle of all of them and refuse to make any plans. I love that!" she joined Scarlett at Lenoir's side. Alice was eventually summoned and the three of them exploded into another love bomb. Hugging and dancing and picking up right where they left off the way only best friends could after four years of being apart. Vincent smiled at them while deciding if he should offer to take everyone out to dinner.

Piper grew bored at their giddiness, for she was a much more sullen teenager than Lenoir had ever been. She grabbed the remote off the coffee table and turned on the television to try and ignore dialog that only made sense to them.

CNN flipped on and the anchor was going on about this John Walker Lindh fellow who had been found to be American fighting in the midst of Al Qaeda. He was from upstate, San Anselmo. They had been going on and on about his traitorous actions for some time now, and how the court of opinion had already convicted him. Vincent watched for a few moments, but then hit Piper playfully on the shoulder, "Turn it off, Piper."

"Come on, there's nothing going on here," she pointed to the giddy quartet who squeaked high pitched syllables.

"There most certainly is," he faked her out and grabbed the remote from her. "We haven't seen your sister in a long time, and we are going to be spending the evening as a family."

"Puke!" Piper rolled her eyes.

Vincent watched the girls, but mostly honed in on his first born while Piper huffed and puffed, exhausted from her boredom. There seemed to be something artificial about

[13]

her. It seemed like a copy of a copy of the real Lenoir. An imitation. As these thoughts flared within him, he felt relief when the girls broke it up and sat back in their respective posts.

"So," the guest of honor began, "tell me what my loving friends and family have been up to. Keep in mind, you've heard from me. While I was off in the light, I was completely in the dark on you."
Vincent and her friends exchanged the slightest of glances, then all tried to talk at once before he motioned for one of them to start.

Of course, it was Scarlett who started. "Casey's back in town," she blurted out.

"Oh?" Lenoir frowned slightly. "How has he been? Where was he?"

Scarlett smiled slyly at her friends, "He's been asking about you a lot. I think he's still hopelessly in love with you."

Lenoir scoffed. "Please, it's been four years! I'm sure he's moved on."

"That's not what I've heard," Ramona jested. "Kimberly Lennon goes to Santa Rosa too, and she told me last year at a Christmas party that he's been holding vigil, waiting for you to come back."

"How about that?" Vincent cut in, "Not even home one hour and you've already got an admirer." He regretted it instantly. It made him sound like somebody's grandfather, and he always hated when his grandfather offered such witticisms when he was a kid.

They looked at him, perplexed, but Ramona continued, "She even said he would move back every summer instead of staying up there, 'just in case Lenoir was back.'"

Lenoir's eyes were wide, but she seemed a little more than disinterested in these revelations. She clicked her tongue, "Poor Casey. I hope Kimberly Lennon was

[14]

mistaken. That's a lot of wasted life. You haven't heard from him, have you dad?"

"I haven't seen him around." Vincent shook his head. "I think the last time I spoke to him was at your graduation party."

The girls, sans Piper, exploded into a fit of laughter once more. It lasted several more minutes and only broke up when Alice emerged from their essence, a tear running down her face from the explosion of emotion, crying out, "I've gotta pee!"

Ramona could hardly contain herself, "I haven't thought about your grad party in soooo long!"

Lenoir laughed weakly and shook her head, repeating, "Poor Casey."

"If you find a man who makes a fool of himself for you, you've found love for life," Scarlett recited.

"What?" Lenoir laughed so hard it looked painful, "You never even liked him!"

"Come on, you can't tell me that hearing this doesn't make you the least bit flattered!"

Alice returned quickly for having to go so bad, "What did I miss out on?"

"Developing a normal sized bladder," Ramona quipped.

Alice shyly sat down and turned slight red.

"So," Vincent started, attempting to steer the conversation away from such silliness. "Speaking of graduation parties, I'll ask you the question everyone asks, 'So what are you going to do now?'"

"Do?" Lenoir glanced out the window down at the valley. The earth had likely eroded somewhat since she last gazed upon it.

"Yeah," Vincent tried to suppress the uneasiness he felt by smiling. "I feel I'd be neglecting my fatherly duty if I didn't ask what your plans are."

"You're going to school, aren't you Lenoir?" Alice asked.

Lenoir stared out the window a moment longer, so much that Vincent felt the inclination to stand up to see if the coyote he had seen hanging around the neighborhood lately had returned. When her eyes came back to them, they were vacant and black. Her formerly light features disappearing along with the setting sun. "School?" She was still lost in whatever thought had changed her. Her ideals oozed from her persona, they were always changing, always waiting to take shape.

"Looks like you should enroll soon," Ramona laughed. "I can hear your brain cells falling over a cliff."

"Rome! She just got back! Can't you see that she's exhausted?" Scarlett smacked her friend on the arm.

"I'm sorry," Lenoir's demeanor took a more serious turn. She looked truly remorseful about something. "It's just a lot to take in at once. All of this."

Even Piper perked up at this sudden change, alerted to the storm raging in her older sister.

But Lenoir swallowed whatever it was that bit her and smiled that plastic smile again. "Absolutely I'm going to school. I've been thinking about getting some generals done. Applying to local schools for Spring and then get serious about a program for next fall."

"I think that's a real smart idea," Vincent admired her decision. "You will need a car to get around in. Maybe when you wake up, we can do some looking. I've cleared my schedule. I can float you some money till you get on your feet. In fact, with the holidays coming up, I could use some extra help around the office. I know you want to make your own way, and this is a way I can help you do it."

Ignoring the obvious contradiction in his statement, Lenoir asked, "Where's my car?"

"The Toyota? Honey, that thing was rusting apart. The neighbors would have started complaining soon. It wasn't safe, and it wasn't going to last long enough for Piper when she gets her license. I had it towed away."

Lenoir got that unoccupied look on her face again.

"I received some money for it though," Vincent lied. "I even invested it for you so that you'd have something to come back to. You can use it to get a new car or use it however you want. It's yours."

She looked thoughtful as she considered what he said, "I think I could use some more of that tea now."

The welcome home party moved into the kitchen. Everyone had a second round of tea, along with some leftover scones David had bought for a social gathering he hosted the previous week for clients. The late autumn light was fading out the window fast, but no one bothered to turn on any lights. They only sat and talked with less emotion and conviction than in the sunroom. Everyone was getting tired, and the novelty of Lenoir's quiet exhaustion was wearing.

Finally, after Piper's pacing, and Scarlett's humming while she chomped on her third scone, Lenoir seemed to find her way out of meandering thoughts. "About the car, dad. Don't worry about it. Like you said, I will make my own way."

"You always have," he smiled proudly at her.

"It must be exhausting to have a daughter like me. I'm sorry I cause you such trouble."

"No," he laughed, "she's the exhausting one," he pointed to Piper who stopped her pacing when she realized everyone was looking at her.

"You guys are weird," she rolled her eyes while singing a nameless tune to herself.

Lenoir approached her and hugged her again more mightily. "No, she's the cute one. We are going to have so much fun together, kiddo."

Piper stopped her singing but didn't look her sister in the eye as a melancholy expression came to her face. "We were worried about you."

"I'm back now. Better than ever."

A chill went down Vincent's spine, it caused him to break the spell of darkness and flip on the kitchen switch as if it would somehow warm things.

"Especially after what happened last year," Scarlett stated in a rare serious tone.

Everyone nodded in sullen agreement.

"Everyone was acting so ridiculous after that," Lenoir explained. "Either they were so sorry for me and what happened to 'my country' or they secretly hated me. The whole thing was just so misguided. Those men, there was no light in their eyes and no love in their hearts."

They stared at her, waiting for her to continue.

"They knew I was American. No matter how hard I tried to hide it after that. They knew I was this or that, whatever it was they thought of people who looked like me. They knew..."

"We were just glad you weren't in any danger," Ramona said, looking puzzled. "Sorry I was calling so much after that, Mr. Adams. I probably drove you crazy. I just knew if she were in trouble, she'd call you."

"I think we were all going a little crazy after that. I couldn't blame you."

Lenoir stared at them, seeming frustrated. Slightly agitated that they couldn't understand what she was trying to get across— or perhaps she was remembering a time she was in danger and decided not to share. Whatever it was, something was alarming her more than she let on, and they all sensed it.

But only Piper was the one to call any attention to it. "Are you all right?"

As if something inside her switched on, some kind of automatic response that sent a zap to the part of her that wasn't spinning her wheels, the strange smile returned. "Oh fine. I think you guys are right, I think I'm more tired than I realized. This place just feels different than it used to."

"Maybe you're different. It has been four years, Noir," Ramona said, not unkindly.

"You're right," she nodded.

"We can leave if you're tired. I've got to be heading back to school anyway. I have a meeting with my Lab group on Monday," Alice explained.

"Are you guys going back soon?"

"My semester is over in just a few weeks," Ramona said. "I'll be back."

"Yeah, me too, then Christmas is right around the corner," Scarlett agreed. "What about you? You're not running off to join Greenpeace or anything any time soon, are you?"

The exhaustion had a full grasp on her now, she was only able to crack a smile. "I'll be around."

She walked her friends to the door, while Vincent and Piper stayed back in the kitchen. Piper seemed less fidgety and more concerned than before. "Is she okay, dad?"

Vincent waved his hand, "Yeah, Pipe. She'll be just fine. She's so tired. It takes a lot out of you— travelling..." he trailed off. The stone sinking deeper in his stomach responded that his youngest may have a point. He watched Lenoir hug her friends goodbye and wondered if she still had what drove her to travel the world in the first place. She seemed to have lost something, and he wondered if that was it. Vincent wasn't naïve enough to realize that as people age into adulthood they tend to lose a few things – preconceived notions about the world, ideals, etc. But as a parent, it gave him a helpless feeling to see it in motion.

He watched her shuffle back to the kitchen, her long ankle length skirt moved breezily as if the stiff November wind outside had somehow travelled through the walls. It

[19]

sent that same chill right back down his spine. "Your bed is all made up for you. Your room is just how you left it."

"Thanks dad," she fell into him and hugged with more might than looked possible from her frail frame.

"Going to bed now, kiddo. You going to be around in the morning?" she asked Piper.

"I don't get up until afternoon on Sundays," she looked warily at her.

"I probably won't either. We'll catch up at lunch then."

"Good night, Lenoir," Vincent called to her.

"Good night," she mumbled. She traipsed like a zombie toward the stairway. "Time to fly away now."

Vincent shuddered, remembering the last time they had spoken in the kitchen and she had said something similar. He focused so much on that moment from the distant past that he hardly heard Piper talking in his ear.

"Dad?!" she asked annoyed.

"Hmmm," he thought he must have sounded like Lenoir at that moment, completely unaware and lost in some kind of fever dream.

"I said, do you care if I watch TV now?"

"Oh," he swallowed, feeling prickly needles in his throat. "No, you go right ahead. Enjoy."

The fight they had four years ago was awful. They argued about college, Vincent was insistent she enroll, and she wouldn't hear it, telling him that world experience is what she needed and then more knowledge to confirm those experiences. He told her he was still her father and she had to obey him. She laughed at him and said he'd have to clip her wings, because she is flying away. The thing that had prompted the argument was her passport showing up in the mail that day. She had threatened it plenty beforehand, but he didn't take it seriously until her smiling face showed up in that little, blue pocket-sized book. It was then he knew he had lost a part of her he would never regain.

[20]

He was bound and determined to never let it happen again.

Part 2

Alive in Purgatory

So where are you now?

You are at the place you have arrived. The goodbye place. A forgone conclusion that had once objected, but now concedes its farewell. For when you step out on that stage, the inquiries will be numerous, yet the answers will restore the bright hope that has always been appreciated, but seldom ever appeared. What is this place?

It's purgatory. Barzakh. The in-between place.

Funny, you never thought it so ordinary.

There is sightlessness here, obscurity in the depths of those around you. They are content, but you have moved on. The plane that has accepted you is not on their radar, nor will it be until you have achieved what you came for. They told you that you are their most important ally. The one to bring it all together. The others that will come after will whisper your name up on the hills, coaxing it to travel along the wind. Your name will be carried, always in the bright light, guarding the temple of Maakan.

So, this is your waiting place. Your dressing room. The place that comes between yesterday's sacrifices and tomorrow's ceremonies. The mystification you feel here is exactly the kind you wish to undo. This cavernous den of mankind's failures, it is up to you to knock down its walls, taste the first breath of fresh air and let in the light. So they can see.

They will assist you in this, they just don't know it yet. They will ask you of your experiences and you will try to recount them, but it will be far beyond reason— perhaps beyond forgiveness. You have forgiven them and have flown higher. You are the one to them to Isik. No one else. You are the perfect shepherd, they told you so.

While this may all feel familiar-- comfortable even, it is not the place you remember. That place's light extinguished long ago, just like the dim flame within you before they rekindled your purpose. While this place's memory remains intact, its purpose has failed. The lives you've touched will not be forgotten, nor will their spirits.

You are their way out of the dark. The way into Rājya. Altogether, all for us, all for them, all for you.

You cannot be preoccupied with the temporary or interim, only the permanent and inevitable. The light will sustain, not the darkness. You and the others, you have found the place to cast your light. It is up to them to see it. Do not fear for them walking toward the unknown. Be proud of the similar place you have walked and took hold.

Where are you? You are at the home of your forgone life, and at the doorstep of the one that is eternal.

Vincent couldn't concentrate. He saw the cursor blinking at him on his monitor, but he had no idea how to respond to it. It was a simple expense report, but his mind stalled and his heart paused at the mere thought of pursuing it. It had been that way ever since she returned.

At first, he had chalked it up to jetlag. Then after another couple days, he thought it was her way of reconciling after being in such a different world for so long. After hearing many of her stories, which ranged from confounding to frightening, he tried to picture her in the places she described. He saw her flowing hair peeking out the back of a hajib. The marketplaces that brought forth the aroma of smoke, fish and the people themselves. Their food, languages and customs perfumed out of their pores. In these visions of her, a stranger in a strange land, he saw her lost in a sea of people. Waiting. Waiting to come back home and continue what he always hoped she would.

A phone rang its double toned ring somewhere back in the office. Papers rustled, the keys on the keyboard clacked to the sound of all the faceless people who had no clear motives, swirling around his daughter. They encompassed her in their impenetrable clutches, getting ready to fly her away again. He stared down at his own office phone, hoping it would sound off to distract him from these daydreams. Then, another thought came to him, as if he had been looking for an excuse to exercise it all along.

He slammed the cradle of his earpiece toward his ear so hard he heard another kind of ring. The sound reverberated as he dialed a number he thought he long since forgotten, all while wondering what she was doing back at home. He pictured Lenoir, curled up on the couch, reading one of the many books she had shipped back. Or maybe she was homesick for a little American TV, but he could only picture her disgusted at the daytime drivel once she powered up the remote.

[25]

Another voice interrupted his train of thought and the sounds that accompanied it, it was Dr. Cassok. He had called his office for a reason, but when his smooth voice repeated h*ello?* he couldn't remember what that reason was.

"Must be a bad connection," the doctor whispered to himself.

"No no, I'm here!" Vincent centered himself back to that moment.

"Whom may I ask is calling?" Dr. Cassok asked, sounding a little more than annoyed.

"I'm sorry, doctor. It's Vincent, Vincent Adams."

There was a slight hesitation and a whispered huff. "Vincent Adams!? It has been a while. How is everything? Is Piper okay?"

Vincent's palms had started to sweat. *What a dumb idea calling the doctor, what good is he going to do? What good did he ever do Piper? Or you? You think he is going to break the hardest stone in the family with such a weak swing?*

"Piper's just fine. She's really happy now. She's happy to have her sister back."

"Oh? Lenoir is back, eh? Just a visit or for good?" He fidgeted with something on his desk or nearby.

"For good, we hope. I wish I knew where she kept her passport so I could say for certain. But you know— daughters."

"Don't remind me," he laughed. "I only have four of them at home. Between them and their mother, I don't stand a chance."

Vincent laughed politely. It was a laugh that reminded him how far off the map Lenoir's own smile, laughter and anything that used to resemble joy had been.

When he thought about what to say next for too long, Dr. Cassok interjected, "So Vincent, it's good to hear from you. I'm glad to hear that Piper is doing well."

"Of course." He swallowed a dry lump.

[26]

"If there isn't anything else, I do have an appointment coming up that I have to prepare-"

"It's Lenoir."

"Okay, what about her?" he remained patient.

"She's not the same as when she left," Vincent turned red when his voice trembled.

"I'm not being facetious mind you, but few people are the same after—how many years was she abroad?"

"Four years."

"Few people are the same after four years, Vincent. Could you be more specific?"

"It's everything about her. I just have this underlying feeling that something terrible has happened to her and she is in some kind of shock because of it. That at least would make sense, that at least would explain her—unusual attitude." He paused, waiting for the doctor to bail him out. When that didn't happen, he thought of something else. "It seems like she's waiting for something. And that is strange for Lenoir. Every action she ever took had a purpose. She's not like me or Piper. She is like her mom though, and I knew when something was wrong with her too."

"I see," Dr. Cassok drew in a breath. "I have to say Vincent, that all seems typically normal."

"It does?" he asked faintly.

"Yes. What else is normal is that when young people return from long trips of independence and are thrust back into a situation where it seems that independence might be threatened, they tend to push a little harder to assert their lack of need for you. The fact that she likely experienced different cultures and different ways of life probably altered her ideals a little bit. That is a phase that soon passes. The longer a person is gone from their typical situation, the longer it takes for them to come back from it. Does that make sense?"

"I suppose it does."

"Is Lenoir making a show of independence?"

[27]

Vincent thought about it and began to laugh. It was a wheezy, uncertain nervous laughter that probably sounded even worse than he imagined. He wanted to scream *yes*, but he didn't know which story to back it up with. He could tell the doctor about the time she was seven and took the car for a spin around the block because she had drawn a picture of her own driver's license. Or he could tell the story of her second day of fourth grade when she informed him she was getting a job because she was smarter than her new teacher who mispronounced her name. There was also the time he received a call from a broker, a man he never met in his life, who said she was in his office, insisting he allow her to buy 300 shares of a company called GammaTech because she had an inside tip. The list went on and on, sometimes Vincent swore she was born at 30 years old. *But how can you explain Lenoir to someone who has never met her?* It seemed impossible. Even more so, the longer he laughed, the more uncertain he was about how to proceed next.

Dr. Cassok remained patient for as long as he could, "Look Vincent, it sounds like you could use a few days off. I think we all get stressed, especially around the holidays. Think about what I said, those at an impressionable age may seem to take longer to adjust to new surroundings, but it is only temporary. I also think you should attempt to back off a little. Your attempts to purify her will only drive her further away. So be careful of how hard you push. Take some time for yourself, relax. If she still seems not herself in a couple of weeks, tell her to make an appointment and I can certainly talk with her. I just think you need to give it a little more time."

"But it feels like I'm in PURGATORY-- all this waiting!" Vincent screamed, shocking himself as much as the ever-patient Dr. Cassok. Not to mention the half of his employees nearest his office that heard.

"Give Piper my best too. Happy holidays, Vincent," Dr. Cassok replied cheerily and disconnected the line.

Vincent stood up, letting the blood that had swelled in his head slowly cascade down to his legs, which felt wooden and rubbery at the same time. He had broken out in a sweat. He looked behind him, out his office door. His assistant and many of the sales force were standing at their desks. Even Mr. Nacey, his newest researcher had his headset dangling at his hip. No one said anything while Vincent smiled politely. He calmly faced his expense report, shut down his workstation, grabbed his coat and case and walked out of the office without saying a word. He drove the long way home. He wasn't sure the route because it was one he had never driven before, but he was far too distracted to be concerned with traffic navigations. He thought about Lenoir and what was driving him so crazy about her. She hadn't done anything, per say. She had said some questionable things, but what twenty-two-year-old doesn't?

After an undetermined amount of time, he switched on some talk radio. The host was ranting about John Walker Lindh again, he seemed to be the prized side topic of the last couple of weeks as the war on terror raged on. The host prattled on and on, *and he knew. He knew about the Qala-i-Jangi uprising. He knew what time it was going to occur, he knew what it would entail, and he said nothing. Nothing but* I'm Irish. *Well folks, your humble host and narrator is also Irish and this kind of backfisted diversion offends me to no end. It offends my Irish ancestry, and it offends my American heritage. This man is a traitor, and we need to try him like a traitor. In this day and age folks, we have to be more vigilant. Someone must have known something about this misguided fool! Someone could have prevented even more American lives from perishing if they only would've thought to say something. But they didn't say something. They just sat back and waited. They are just as guilty as Lindh if you ask me.*

Vincent switched the radio back off. The sweat continued to pour from his head which now also throbbed. After more miles, the sun began to set an instance or two sooner than it had the previous night. Without even trying, Vincent was back driving in his upper middle-class neighborhood. The cracked concrete sidewalks had given way to newly paved trails. The taxis and food stands slowly migrated into Benz's and bistros.

Then something strange caught his eye, when he pulled up to his gate on Cannon Drive. A strange boy was walking away from it. He supposed he could have come from further up the block, but Vincent swore he was walking away from the gate in front of his house. It could have been a friend of Lenoir's; once word got out that she was back, she had had all sorts of visitors. Friends from school, pen pals, cousins, the people she used to volunteer with– everyone wanted to see her again.
This boy was different though. He looked unfamiliar and had a strange sense of purpose and demeanor. He walked straight ahead, seeming unaware of what he was doing. The boy was likely older than he looked on account of the confidence that came with his stride. A long white robed was draped over his skinny frame. Vincent couldn't see his shoes, but the way he walked, he might as well have been levitating a couple of inches off the ground. Finally, having an inclination on something he could control, Vincent squealed his tires as he violently pulled to the curb to get a better look. He rolled down his window, it had gotten cold since the sun went down. His breath was slightly visible as he awaited the boy, who seemed to take no notice.

He watched him pass without saying a word. The boy looked straight ahead as if Vincent wasn't even there at all. It made him feel like a ghost in a world that used to be his but was disappearing one memory at a time. Vincent thought about calling him over for a neighborly chat and to dig up some information, but a flashing light inside his

[30]

home distracted him. It looked as if Lenoir were having guests over after all.

As he maneuvered his car back toward the right side of the two-way street, he noticed something else. A black van was parked further up the hill. It was noticeable instantly on account that very few cars ever parked on the street in his neighborhood. There was a shadow in the van he could see through the windshield. A couple of cigarette butts lay next to the van's door. Someone was watching.

Probably those idiots who are renting the Miller's summer home, his mind remembered. They were a couple of presumably spoiled college kids who had moved in around Labor Day. Vincent thought they looked shady and warned Piper to steer clear of them. He had seen strange cars circling the block recently too. Probably dealing drugs or running an illegal gaming operation or whatever it is that puts hair on the balls of adolescents now days. It relieved him a little, because of course his first thought went straight to Lenoir.

"What do you think she's mixed up in?" he muttered to himself as he entered the passcode for the gate and started up the driveway. *Danger*, his mind answered.

Maybe Dr. Cassok was right, he thought, calming a bit more at the absurd degree of his paranoia. *You just have to give it a little more time, she'll come around. You are forgetting whose daughter she is.*

After gathering his belongings from the day, he slowly ambled up to the front door and slipped inside.

It was like walking through a portal into another dimension. Sometime between when Vincent had left that morning and returned, Lenoir took it upon herself to redecorate the sunroom and a large majority of the kitchen. She had her grandmother's old afghan's draped over the sofas. She had her old glow in the dark sheets that displayed different constellations hung from the ceiling, creating a strange path of dividers that rendered the entire

[31]

room a maze. Incense burned in the corner, which he suspected was camouflage for another more mind-altering smell. But instead, large wafts of food he had never inhaled before invaded his senses. Some of it was burning, the rest was encrusted to his late wife's fine china that was strewn across end tables and a decorative piece given to him by a co-worker years ago.

Annoyed and relieved all at the same time, he picked up the plate and leveled it when the concoction of chickpeas, rice and what looked like minced beef started sliding down the side. He heard voices of both men and women, they were speaking in relaxed droning tones that were a bit off putting. Strange, exotic music blared off in directions impossible to pinpoint on account of the maze of sheets.

After placing his belongings on the stairwell, Vincent ventured back into the sunroom to try and locate his daughter. He started lifting back sheets when maneuvering the maze was not working. He spotted a couple of his nieces and nephews and made cordial greetings to them. In another cordoned off area, he found a boy he had never seen in his life with his shirt off and a girl giving him a massage. They looked surprised to see him, but they made no attempt in hiding their actions. Vincent only huffed, rolled his eyes and moved on. The wild music blaring a combination of percussion, stringed and wind instruments was hard to hear over, but he started calling her name anyway.

"Lenoir? Oh daughter dearest!"

He paused when he found the trove of incense. There was a large pile of it in a flat ashtray with a big peace symbol in the middle of it. He was pretty sure his late wife had owned it too at one point but had no idea it was still around. "Hey Noir?"

He heard a familiar voice he thought belonged to his daughter, it was accompanied by a softer voice in which he may have also been acquainted.

[32]

"I don't know, Noir. This whole thing seems kind of weird. What was with that guy in the robe? I thought we were going to look through college catalogs?"

"Come on, Alice," it was most certainly his daughter's voice. "You were said to have an open mind. There are some really beautiful ideas in here," this was followed by a tapping noise.

"I don't know. I think I should go," Alice answered, sounding upset.

Once he rounded a corner of a sheet displaying Andromeda, he wandered into their nook. "Hey girls," he announced himself, "having fun?"

Alice looked up at him, a bit perturbed and surprised to see him, but in a way, almost relived.

Lenoir wore the same empty disposition she came home with, but there was a slight smirk on her face this time. There was a glass of wine within arm's reach, as well as a leather-bound book between the two of them as they sat on the floor. Vincent couldn't get a good look at it. "Me Pitājī? How are thee?" she sang.

"I'm just fine, Lenoir. Just fine. I saw your cousins Rutherford and Isla."

Her eyes widened as she hummed along with the music, "Are they still here? I thought they'd gone."

"Who is the guy with his shirt off?"

"Oh, that's Harper. He was a friend of Isla's and Genevieve. She might still be around too. Did you see them?"

"I wouldn't know them. You want to tell them that this isn't a massage parlor?"

"Spoken like a true patriarch," she beamed. "Are you hungry? I made some Falafel and Kebab with spicy tomato."

He tried to ignore the aromas coming from the plate, even though he was starving, he shook his head. "I think maybe we should start wrapping it up, huh Noir?"

"Oh daddy, it is wrapping up. I mean the mariachi band just left," she teased.

"Very funny," he smirked. "Speaking of, what is this you're listening to?"

The horns ceased and gave way to an odd throat piercing chanting that was as relentless as it was frightening. It sounded as if it were meant to hypnotize or extort the soul somehow.

"Oh this?" A more serious look came to her face. "This is *Gnostic Psalter*. It goes all the way back to the second century."

"Is that right?" Vincent was distracted by the sight of a candle that had been carelessly knocked over and not picked up. There was a dried pool of wax on his floor next to it.

"It was something we listened to all the time with the friends I made in Tikr-"

"Look Noir, I've gotta get back," Alice interjected, her brown eyes narrowed.

"What? Come on, I thought you were going to stay over." her voiced pitched in a way that Vincent hadn't heard in a while. It reminded him of a time when her life was more innocent. When everything was less complicated.

Alice shook her head, still upset over what had transpired. "I don't think so. I've got shopping to do tomorrow."

"That's fine, so do I. We can go together."

"I'll call you tomorrow then," Alice pulled away, standing up to leave. "Bye, Mr. Adams."

"Vincent," he reminded her as she sprinted toward the door. Once she slammed it shut, he turned to his daughter, feigning amusement, but worried all over for her. "What did you do to her?"

Lenoir stared back at him, that vacant look he had come to detest, plagued the middle of her face. "Nothing." She sat back down on a dingy looking rug he had no idea where she got. It was embroidered and covered with Aztec looking suns, stars and moons. The fabric at the ends were frayed and shedding lint. She sat down and took a deep breath, holding it for what seemed a long time to Vincent. He started to walk away, but peeked behind the Andromeda sheet at her, watching, waiting to make sure she exhaled and then drew another one back in. She raised her arms up and in front of her in what looked like the toe stand Yoga pose. She hummed again to clear her mind. A breeze blew in from a nearby open window and kissed the sheet, causing it to waver and ripple.

Vincent was brought back in time to a year earlier.

It was in Pakistan, a tiny little airstrip near the town of Konkar, his route to Jinnah International Airport and home to Los Angeles. He had hugged his daughter goodbye on many occasions: summer camps, school trips, but the time at the airstrip in Konkar was the hardest. He remembered viewing her yellow hair dancing in the breeze through teary, stinging eyes. He sensed it even then, the change in her.

Just like he sensed it now, watching her meditate, or gain back the light as she has been stating the last couple of weeks.

What happened to you, Lenoir? He had to bite his lip to keep from asking. As the loud, abrasive music continued in the background and the couple exchanging massages laughed between the hung sheets behind him, Vincent became distraught. More than distraught, he was at his wit's end on how to proceed with his daughter. He knew then that something had happened in that year, and that all her clandestine affairs had affected her in ways he can't possibly understand.

She breathed in and out several more times before he retired to his bedroom, away from the sounds and smells of

[35]

the life she couldn't seem to shake, nor did she want to. While he may not be able to ask her, he could certainly do his own diligence in bringing his daughter back. She was here physically, and he felt as long as she remained present, it was a step in the right direction. Now he just had to figure out how to bring her mind back home.

Later on, while reading a ministry's web page on his laptop in bed, he heard the sound of a knock at the front door. As far as he knew, everyone had vacated the premises after Lenoir had finished her meditation session and what sounded like her offering of a blessing before sending them on their way. He also heard dishes clattering and the fabric ruffling for a period. Even in her absence, she still was the same hard-headed independent that didn't ever need to be asked to tidy up after having guests over. Vincent felt like it was something he had always taken for granted. It would also be something that he would have to battle ferociously-- that willfulness. It would make the forthcoming task of bringing the rest of his daughter back home all the more demanding.

He heard her voice murmuring in soft, unconfident tones. Surprise and abatement trickled from her; he could hear it all the way from upstairs. He tried his best to ignore it, give her her privacy and continue reading a fascinating article on this minister and his travels abroad, freeing captive minds in the Mediterranean. He had thought about sneaking up to the stairwell and listening in. The images of the boy in the robe walking past him down their street and Alice's worried look were still fresh in his mind. But he also remembered what Dr. Cassok had stated, *your attempts to purify her will only drive her further away, so be careful how hard you push.*

Wise words, Vincent thought, re-reading the same line for the fourth time. Then the atmosphere downstairs had taken a left turn, shifting in a way that could only be thought of as intense. He saw her freckled, slightly worried but excited face on that airstrip again. A cloud of dust encircling them as they embraced and the skycap rolling his eyes and waiting ever impatiently for the father and daughter to finish their goodbye.

A shriek from downstairs caused his laptop to land awkwardly on its side as he ripped back the sheets and stormed the hallway. He would have called her name, but his mind was racing a mile per minute, still back in the hot, unforgiving desert as predators seemed to close in and more innocent memories escaped.

Lenoir was talking softly once again, but she was pleading a case, to whom and what about was still a mystery. "You cannot come in right now. My father and sister are home."

"When?"

"No," her voiced raised slightly and the sound of a slight scuffle followed.

"When then? You don't even know what I've been going through without you, Noir. My life has become a sterile environment. It's been completely empty."

"It sounds like you need some light in your life."

"Then teach me how to let it in, Lenoir."

There was the sound of more pushing. Based on what he was hearing, it was likely Casey Arnold, Lenoir's high school boyfriend. Vincent had always liked Casey right from the beginning. Back then, he thought Casey would bring Lenoir down to earth a little bit. Even though he wasn't the sharpest tool, it never seemed to bother him that his love for his daughter bordered on obsession. He was never worried because she knew how to handle herself. It was her current situation that frightened him the most, because it preyed upon her biggest weakness, her virtue.

"Not here, not now," she demanded.

"I'm not leaving until you give me a time and place," he said emotionally.

[37]

"Saturday, coffee, 9AM, Brewed Awakening. After that you have to forget me, Casey."

"It's hard to forget someone who gave you so much to remember," he fled down the driveway. His damp sounding footfalls seemed to fade into the windy, black night.

Lenoir sighed and closed the door.
Vincent stood at the top of the stairway for a moment. Listening to her clean up the remnants of the party. With the click of a remote, on came strange woodwind instruments that sounded like they evaporated from a haunted forest. Sounds of marching feet made up the rhythm and the earthy, ethereal tones of a shrieking chanting voice sent chills throughout an otherwise warm home.

Vincent snapped to it and descended the stairs. She was fluffing the last of the pillows and returning them to their respective spots on the sofa, a perfectly stacked set of folded sheets lay behind her on the coffee table.

"Do you want some tea?" she asked, almost like she was expecting him.

"No thanks," he stared at her. "Everything all right?"

"Fine," that phony, unpopulated smile came to her face again.

"Lenoir, that story you told me a few weeks ago. The one about the barn gathering you attended with the French students."

Then a real smile creased her lips, "the ancient city of Arpamyl. I'll never forget."

"That missionary you joined. They were spiritual, yes?"

"Of course," she frowned slightly.

"You really were just helping the unfortunate?"

"Haven't I always?" she folded her arms, indicating the soup kitchens she volunteered for on Thanksgiving

[38]

nights, the bell ringing for the salvation army at Christmas, the summer she spent as a youth camp counselor at Mt. Cross.

"I'm not doubting your philanthropy. I never have. I've always known you as nothing but a modern-day Sabine Gould. I just wanted to know."

Ask her his mind screamed at him. *Ask her before it's too late. How many stories have you seen and read about parents wishing they would have reached out directly after tragedy.*

"What?" she looked genuinely perplexed and worried about him.
"Should I be worried? In regards of how you were treated by those you traveled with?"

She smiled the way she did in the desert at him when she whispered *time to fly away now.* "You should be proud. A daughter is a day brighter, and a heart warmer."

She moved on from the topic, glossing over it the way an addict would gloss over missing money once their fix had been administered. She asked if she could make something called *kanafeh* as a dessert for Thanksgiving. She told him of her weekend plans but failed to mention coffee with her high school sweetheart. She explained everything so convincingly that it deflated him all over again. It gave him an eerie feeling of powerlessness against her. He realized he was relegated to the same role poor Casey Arnold had been relegated to. Waiting for Lenoir to come back was like waiting for the sun to burn out. But the waiting was all they had.

Part 3

The Inner Temple of Makaan

So where are you now?

You remain in this nebulous place. You let the water cleanse and overcome you. You have *real* struggles here. Not the kind that can be reversed with gravity or consequence, but with light. For you are the floating contradictory within the eternal nightfall those around you embrace. While you struggle to break through it, they become more immune. They prefer it this way. They need it to be this way.

The light seems to be getting farther and farther away as you sink into your previously habituated abyss. They try to reach for you through their orthodox means, but you can't hear them, for you answer another call. You listen to the voice inside you as you float further out of arm's reach. They can't touch you on the level you can touch them-- let alone fathom the ransom you will pay for their sovereignty.

But there are more variations at play than a mere division of dark and light. As you learned long ago, the world is not a perfect place, only your intentions can make it so. The bottom of this depth is littered with tiny pockets of beams. It reminds you of looking out upon an ocean of stars, admiring their wax and wane, their bursts of energy and luminosity filling you with hope, happiness and joy. What is the source of this light, they may ask? Your radiation of Makaan and the teachings of Isik, you may tell them.

Even your former compatriots have slivers of light beneath their clouded cloaks, but they can't bear to bring them out. Tread carefully, O beautiful soul in breaking through the shells they've spent a lifetime constructing. You may find resistance and horrors unlike you've known in the dark, cold waters of the past.

Your destiny has been elected. Despite your compatriots' woe, your purpose will shine through them. You must reconcile their desires and leave them at peace so they can be afforded your affluences when they too reach Rājya. There they will be at ease and accept your advancement.

In the interim, you will fly high while still weathering the currents at the surface. You will reflect and recount as best you can, the path that led you to your light. Eventually they will tire of your perception, because they will not be able to support it, nor your duty to remain on your path. It is natural for them to scorn what they don't recognize, for remember they live in the shadow.

So where are you in your abyss? You're in the middle of a false-sanctuary, forever misleading and sinking faster from the pressure and weight above you. Fight to look toward the light, and the light will lead you to Makaan. Where are you going? The place. Where will you be when you get there? Home.

"She's heeeere!!!" Courtney, Ramona's well meaning, but spastic little sister announced.

Annoyed, Ramona turned from her friends, Alice and Scarlett who had arrived earlier. She shot an annoyed look toward her skinny, noisy sibling. "Greeaaat," she rolled her mouth along with her eyes, "You did your job. Now why don't you make like the fetus you are and 'head out'!"

Confused, Courtney turned toward her sister's friends for clarification, but was only received with laughter from Scarlett and awkward fidgeting from Alice.

"You should be nicer to your sister," Lenoir grinned when Ramona opened the door, somehow hearing their exchange.

She waved a hand, "Stepsister."

Lenoir held up a brown bag, "I brought wine. I also brought something else I want you all to try."

"Oh boy," Ramona replied sarcastically.

"I haven't even told you what it is yet," the smile remained as she waltzed in with her purse, an overnight bag and her bedroll all tucked neatly under her arm.

"You want some help with that?" Alice still spoke to Lenoir with kid gloves, as if she were volatile or unstable. It annoyed Ramona to no end. Just before Noir had arrived, Alice was going on about how something had changed with her, and she felt like she was the only one to see it. She had warned both Ramona and Scarlett to be on the lookout for anything out of the ordinary. Her words, as if there was such a thing as ordinary when it came to Lenoir. Alice talked as if she were a psychopath who was just let out of an institution, but still untrustworthy, despite her release. Sometimes Alice's anxiousness and unfounded fears chided her to no end.

"I got it, thank you though," she slipped her clogs off in one smooth motion. "Can I pop this stuff into the fridge?"

"You know where it is," Ramona outstretched an arm. "We started a bottle here already so grab yourself a glass too."

"You bet," Noir smiled warmly and winked.

As soon as she left the foyer, the worried look on Alice's face returned, "You see?"

"What Alice? Jesus."

"That was so phony. You can see what's underneath it all, can't you? She is obviously hurting, or in some kind of shock about something."

"She probably realized what she's in for spending the evening with such a wet blanket," she scolded.

"This is serious," Alice persisted. "I just want someone else to see what I see."

Ramona huffed, her brown bangs thrusting forward, she was trying to remain patient, "I thought you were supposed to be over the whole second-year syndrome thing by now."

"This was such a good idea, Ramona," Scarlett piped in in a sing-songy voice, either because she was uncomfortable, which amused Ramona, or because she was already drunk. "An old-fashioned sleep over, just like we used to."

"I just figured it was a special occasion," she replied, not knowing how to take the praise.

Lenoir floated back in with her coat off and a wine glass held out.

Alice snapped back to attention, not wanting to tip her hand, and Ramona gave her a glance that asked *now who is being phony?*

Ramona handled the hosting duties well enough, pouring Noir a glass that killed the first bottle, and turning on the radio, *Dave Matthews*, to find some background music.

"Together again," Lenoir eased back into a beanbag chair Ramona had on the floor of her main level. Some kind of entertainment show was on the television in the

[44]

background that dished on all the latest celebrity gossip. She was pretty sure it was the result of Scarlett holding the remote, the only one who cared about such things.

"Besides when you came back, when was the last time that happened?" Scarlett beamed.

"Too long," Ramona agreed, punctuating the initial stilted mood she was determined Alice had set.

Things were awkward for the first round of topics until the conversation and wine found their footing. It was then Scarlett who produced a familiar looking green bottle out of her overnight bag. "Who's up for something slightly more potent?" The grin on her face turning devilish as strange moonlight and the glow from the Christmas lights on Ramona's house slipped in from outside.

Ramona lit up at the sight of it, her cheeks flushed and for the first time since Noir arrived, she was able to shove Alice's words from her mind. "I'll enlist."

"Do you know what that stuff does to your heart?" Alice scrunched her pale cheeks.

"I'm sorry," Ramona replied sardonically, "can I get you a Zima?"

More giggles ensued; even Alice looked like she had loosened up a bit.

"Shots? Or do you want a mixer?" Scarlett asked, pleased to have a partner in crime.

"From the bottle," Ramona stated triumphantly before remembering her other guest. "Noir?"

"Maybe after the wine," she pointed to her glass. The TLC song, *Waterfalls,* a song Ramona had nearly forgotten came to life on the radio. "Oh my god!" she choked down her first shot of Jägermeister once she realized the connection.

"Wow, nostalgia overload!" Scarlett sat up from the floor, her blue eyes dancing.

"What?" Lenoir wondered aloud.

[45]

"Please tell me you haven't forgotten about us completely," Ramona gave her a strange look.

"You really don't remember?" Scarlett asked.

"The talent show?" Alice finished.

She was lost for another moment, searching her memories—searching so hard she nearly lost herself.

It could have been because of Alice's fidgeting beside her, but Ramona was terrified that if Lenoir could not come up with the memory, it would only serve to validate Alice's theory. Feeling the warm tingly sensation of the Jag sliding down her tract, she silently cheered for her friend and her ability to conjure up the moment.

It was evident the minute it came to her. Swallowing her last sip of wine, she nearly spit it back out when the memory reintroduced itself. She began laughing so hard it sounded like she was crying. This allowed the others to join in and partake. Even Alice joined in mimicking the uncoordinated moments of them trying to perform the song up on the stage of the school auditorium in front of their dismayed classmates.

"Maybe we should have practiced a little bit," Scarlett squealed, her bleached locks swirling along with her body.

"You think?" Ramona chortled.

"You two and the wrong verse," Alice pointed hysterically.

"Us? What about you and *my bloody only hope...*" Ramona said. "We were like, what is this? The vagina Star Wars monologues?"

"Remember when Adam Barclay tried to start booing us off stage?" Alice tittered.

"Yeah, until Casey started pounding on him because he was so in love with Lenoir. Ha-ha! Still is, I guess."

This quieted the group considerably. It allowed TLC in the background to retake center stage, edging out the faded image of the group making complete fools of themselves in some kind of rowdy ode to MTV.

Lenoir looked down at her empty glass, likely deciding whether to excuse herself to refill it. The smile remained on her face like a leftover scar, but she looked genuinely sad about something.

Ramona noticed Alice picking up on it as well, and before she could ruin it by saying something to bring them down further, she asked, "Have you seen Casey at all? Has he heard you're back in town?"

"He knows," Noir responded whimsically, her voice not matching her sad eyed face at all.

"Sounds like there's a story there."

She nodded and looked up to face them, a smirk remained creased in one corner of her mouth.

"Spill it," Ramona demanded.

"Maybe I will take a shot of that Jag after all," she laughed nervously, which invited more snickering.

"Did you see him?" Scarlett asked, antsy.

Lenoir nodded again as she downed the shot of Jägermeister with a loud gulp and squeamish look. "Blech! It tastes nothing like it used to. I just thought of something. Is this the first time we've all drank together? I suppose it must be."

"Legally anyway. But quit stalling and dish on Casey," Ramona kept her in check.

She cleared her throat, "It's like swallowing molten glass fragments."

Scarlett snickered, "Where did you see him?"

"I met him for coffee a couple weeks ago."

"How'd it go?" Alice asked.

"That boy is hopeless."

Another burst of laughter erupted from Ramona's den, although it was less explosive than before. From Ramona's view, they all felt for Casey, a lost romantic still in love with his high school crush. There was something sweet and sad about it at the same time, and even though she hated the thought because it brought back a host of other memories, Ramona felt a little envious that Lenoir had someone pining after her.

In response to this troubling recollection, Ramona still gripped the Jägermeister bottle tightly and took a large swig. She belched halfway through, nearly sending hot streaks of liquid fire streaming down her cheeks. She exhaled nervously and felt the pleasant warm fever sweep across her again, a bit more intensely than before.

"What did he say?" Alice persisted.

"He spent most of the forty-five minutes I gave him explaining how his life has been a large black hole since I left. How he tried to fill that hole with all sorts of things, but the hole only wants one thing."

"You?" Ramona smirked.

"Bingo," Lenoir flushed, a rare looking embarrassment crossing her face. "I guess I'm the only thing this abyss can be plugged with. I guess I have to fill his hole."

"Huh, with most guys it's the other way around, but that Casey always went his own way," Scarlett quipped.

A heartier, more stinging laughter followed, it caused Ramona's muscles to squeeze worse than a menstrual cramp. The room shook so much it caused wide reaching decibels to slam against their ears. The waves of sound even seemed to cause the outline of the objects on her mother's free-standing cabinet to bend and contort in ways physically impossible. It was then, as the blood rushed in and out of Ramona's head, that she realized she was bombed.

Once the last fit died down, Alice asked, "What did you tell him?"

"Tell him?" Lenoir wrinkled her forehead. "I told him it was not my responsibility to light his path and that each of us needs to find our way ourselves. He understood that and tried to counter with the two hearts are better than one mantra. I just told him that we are in different places, and that we achieved all we could together during our time and place. He didn't understand that. He didn't want to understand that. He lives in an empty world. One where only the ghosts of the past keep him company. You know what I mean?"

The girls shifted in their seats but said little. Alice's concerned look returned, but Ramona and Scarlett, passing the bottle back and forth were brimming with something more jubilant.

"So, did he accept that? I don't think so," Lenoir continued. "I told him if he loves me like he says he does, he will respect my decision. When that didn't stick, I simply said that my heart belongs to another now. Then he got mad, told me I was afraid of commitment or something to that effect and blamed me for wasting his life." She sighed, puffing her cheeks before adding, "I want him to be happy. Maybe I should have told him that, but he just would have kept coming back. Better to let him down all the way, right?"

"So, it's true?" Scarlett questioned.

"What is?"

"That your heart belongs to another?" she grinned.

"I had to tell him something."

To which Scarlett started ooing and ahhing like a seven-year-old incapable of understanding the emotions involved. Trying to keep the mood light and euphoric, Ramona figured it was a good time to join her.

Lenoir raised an eyebrow, surprised or startled by their maturity, but then laughed, likely realizing their joyful drunkenness had spread to each of them by way of the Jägermeister.

"You met him on your trip, didn't you?" Alice asked, a whisper of apprehension still in her voice, even after her second glass of wine.

"I told you there was nothing to worry about," Ramona slapped Alice's shoulder.

"Met who?" Lenoir asked, doing a good job sounding confused.

"Forget it, bitch. You're busted," Ramona bullied. "Tell us about him."

Lenoir glanced at each of them and seemed to realize something about their fragmented exchange. She relaxed, refilled her glass with the fresh bottle Scarlett had brought out and reflected on something proudly, even joyously. It was the happiest Ramona had seen her since she had returned, and there was something off about that happiness. It seemed to come from the same place that Casey's yearning for Lenoir did. It seemed wrong somehow. But alas, her mind was not able to hold onto the thought for long when Scarlett, who grew bored with waiting for the details to start singing *Waterfalls* all over again, only it was the sloppiest rendition she had ever heard.

"I think her face says it all," Ramona teased after Lenoir clammed up.

"At least tell us his name," Scarlett begged.

"And if he's a good kisser," Alice added, to which the others turned to her in surprise until they were squealing and rolling on the floor again.

"If you're still talking about Casey, he's all yours," Noir's face turned red as it looked like her lungs had momentarily forgotten how to breathe.

"I don't want him!" Alice gasped, shaking her head.

When that tirade died down and glasses were again refreshed, Lenoir came clean. "His name is Isik Veren," that strange look of delirium smothered her face once more.

Her friends all cheered in unison, performing a variety of wooden hand movements that approved of this new union. Then, all at once, they shushed themselves in order for her to continue.

She looked at all of them, minding them with a certain caution. Ramona supposed it was because she was carefully pouring over her thoughts so they came out in just the right way.

Lenoir swirled the wine in her glass, creating a small tornado that burped air bubbles until she placed it back on her coaster. "I met him at Makaan. *The Place*, is what we'd call it."

"A club?" Scarlett assumed. "What kind of music? House? Trip-hop? Good drinks?" she fired off the questions in four-shot bursts.

"It wasn't like that," Noir shook her head.

"What was it like?" Ramona asked again, growing tired of the foreshadowing.

"It was a temple. A big, beautiful temple. Ceilings as high as a museum, but filled to the brim with people, just like me."

"Americans?" Alice asked.

"No, people that were searching for something. Now, I've been to many temples before, they all promised one thing or another. There were so many charlatans in the Maraan district you half expected to be offered Rolexes and boot-legged movies at every corner."

"What were you searching for?" Alice asked.

Lenoir Adams took a deep breath, the wind whistled in from outside. A breeze blew somewhere out there colder than it intended. It caused the Christmas lights outside Ramona's house to bask the den in a strange looping glow that gave the moment a more ominous tone. "I didn't know it at the time, but I was searching for the light."

Ramona snorted as if it were a really hilarious joke. However, no one else moved a muscle, waiting for more details before passing judgement.

"I wish there was a way to make you all understand, but words really don't do it justice." She sighed, frustrated, taking another sip of wine.

They stayed silent, waiting for a revelation.

"I got it!" Lenoir roared. "Close your eyes and I'll tell you." A Macy Gray song came on the radio while the three fulfilled their old friend's request. Alice squinted hard, her trepidation seemed to come back to her in waves. Scarlett had a big grin on her face as she peacefully shut her lids, swaying in semi circles as she sat Indian style on the floor. Ramona, hesitant at first, finally closed hers too, thinking how dumb the whole conversation was, wishing instead she had introduced a game like *Charades* or even *Truth or Dare*. "So, there you are walking into this temple that looks like a set piece from *Lawrence of Arabia*," she began. Beautiful high ceilings that look like otherworldly Roman Steeples, sand underfoot so fine that all the blisters you developed over the many months of walking seemed to melt right off your toes. Right away you notice something in this place. This temple of Maakan. A feeling you get deep in the corners of your happiest filaments. A riff of a couple of chords play somewhere off in the distance, nothing fancy, minor chords you've probably heard ten thousand times before. Only now they take on a whole new kind of meaning. The instrument is something between an organ and a harpsichord. It carries you away while bringing you closer to it all at the same time.

"At first, you're afraid. Large men patrol the area, they have long robes of 'abyad on, the sand seems to glisten off them. There is a purity in the air that smells of sage and tathir. At first you are afraid. Deeply afraid. It feels like you have desecrated something by even stepping foot inside. But they look at you like no one has ever looked at you before. And slowly their light begins to shine. The way they look at you makes you feel like the most beautiful thing in the world. As the faces of each man and woman come into focus, they seem to be getting farther away before they get closer. Even though the land that surrounds this temple of Maakan is shrouded in tyranny, Makaan itself is free, and you can feel it in every artifact you touch. Taste it in every

[52]

offering they give you. You felt the feeling for years, but you never recognized it for what it is, for what it means to you.

"You get the feeling of goodbye, a sad and stringent feeling, yet it feels like you are getting closer still to the light. With the music, the soft inviting chanting, the way they look at you. You are powerless to accept anything less. You aren't just saying goodbye to everything you thought was true about the world, your saying goodbye to everything because everything is different now. In just a look, they change your whole perspective of the world, but that's not all. Isik Veren approaches you slowly, softly, his piercing eyes make you feel like you are the only thing in the world that's come from such a dark place. You feel yourself blossoming, the fate of a thousand seasons flowing through you, and it is the most powerful thing.

"Your able to croak a phrase, just one, a phrase you never thought you even knew. You whisper it softly as he approaches, his hands out in front of him. *Mae alssalama.*

"Then he does it, but there is no fear, there is quite the opposite. As he puts his hands on you for the first and only time, you then realize what you have been looking for. You can see it. It is blinding and beautiful. You close your eyes real tight, but it has already infiltrated you. The light in your eyes will never subside. It will only grow brighter from every day onward.

"It's not about Isik Veren at all. He's just an intermediary. It has and always will be about the light. The people's eternal light."

She paused. For a moment, even though she resisted opening her eyes, Ramona thought she may have left the room, but then she heard her breathing beside her. She felt a tear roll down her cheek. She could feel one thing Lenoir spoke about, the sadness. The meaning of the goodbye. She knew right then and there that things hadn't been the same for a while now, and they probably would never be again.

"Now- open your eyes," Lenoir whispered to them.

Alice also had stained eyes when she opened them, but Scarlett, too far gone from the shots she had prescribed was completely lost. Ramona pushed away the shot she had poured for her, feeling like something was sitting right on her stomach, crushing her lung power. She needed to slow down. Something about Noir's speech had sent ripples of unnerve through her. But at the same time, she was upset with herself for giving it so much credence. If she wasn't careful, she would turn into Alice before you know it. She thought the speech was arrogant. Ramona had a cousin once who spent a semester abroad in Brussels. When she returned, she had an accent, a dreadful haircut and a whole new outlook on life. After six months. The annoyance she felt with her cousin Cassie was the same kind she felt now toward her much better friend, Lenoir. Still, she hoped the moment would pass with some kind of clear-headed revival. She would give her the benefit of the doubt.

"Do you see it?" Lenoir asked them. "I do. I see the light in this place and in all of you." She took another sip of her wine. "Do you know how I know it's real? Let me tell you something I've probably never told you before. A story. It happened a long time ago, when my father was still working at the university. There was this enormous pool there, it dwarfed any pool I had ever been in. I was only six years old. My father let me come in and swim after hours while he sat and worked by the pool. Those were some ridiculously happy times. I was obsessed with the water back then. When it was too cold to swim in the ocean, he would take me to the university where I would splash around for hours until my fingers and toes were numb and pruney.

"Anyway, one particular day he had to leave the room for a moment. I know what you're thinking. Vincent Adams is way too smart and responsible of a parent to leave his six-year-old daughter alone in a pool with almost a million gallons of water, but he did. I don't fault him for it. I haven't talked to him for a while about it, but I bet he just needed to grab something quick, and he'd be right back. However it came to be, he left me in the pool alone. I remember drifting close to the deep end. The bottom seemed a universe away. It was so far below me that it was the color of a coal. The blackness was so mesmerizing I couldn't look away. It seemed to swallow me up. Before I knew it, I was sinking fast and for some reason, I was paralyzed by the darkness I could not even move to swim up to the surface, even though I knew how. I was terrified, sinking fast like a stone, but unable to do anything about it.

"Regardless, Dad came back in and got me out of there. I remember him yelling at me out of frustration. I'm sure he was just frustrated at himself, but I scared the living shit out of him. Ever since that time, I haven't been in a huge hurry to get back in the water. I carried that fear, not of the water itself, but of the eternal blackness around with me for years and years. Every birthday party at a pool or invite to a beach day left me with the same feeling of emptiness and dread. That was until I entered the temple of Maakan. I never thought anything could ever penetrate that darkness, but the eternal light did. It has some kind of power and I know it must sound crazy, but it got inside me and it will stay with me until the day I die."

"Noir," Ramona started, but quickly snapped her mouth shut, unable to think of what to say next. She was more annoyed by the glowering shadow this story and conversation had cast on her party.

Alice's upset won out, it seemed. She sat stewing on the floor, probably trying to rationalize how to kidnap Lenoir and deliver her to the nearest deprogrammer, as if one could be found in the yellow pages.

Scarlett shook the shot glass of Jägermeister that Ramona had left behind, daring her to drink it. She giggled to herself, unable or unwilling to acknowledge anything their mutual friend had said, despite the tone the evening had taken.

Ramona glanced between Lenoir who looked hopefully back at her, and to the shot glass her drunken friend was dangled in front of her face. The golden liquid sloshed over the sides, reducing it to a half a shot. She confiscated the remnants from Scarlett before giving it a second thought, downing what turned out to be nothing more than a couple of drops.

Lenoir, unfazed by her response dug something out of her overnight bag. It was a leather-bound book that had no cover and no writings on the front. It was loosely bound and worn at the corners. She opened it to a pre-marked page and began reading in a language foreign to everyone else in the room. This action visibly upset Alice even more, to which Lenoir began to rub her shoulder, effortlessly crawling down onto the floor next to her, yet continued reciting the passages.

Ramona had enough of the spectacle. She rolled her eyes, letting the somber sisters enjoy each other's company. She'd rather be interacting with the bubbly, if not slightly brainless Scarlett. At least she was expressing emotions Ramona could connect with. So, she poured them each another shot of Jägermeister, stopping long enough to admire how much of the bottle they had killed. Letting the uncomfortable moment Noir had created slip behind and away from her. She knew the headache in the morning would hurt, but she didn't care. Anything to get away from that feeling. It was the same one she felt when her parents had split up all those years ago. So, Scarlett and Ramona poured drinks like there was no tomorrow. When the inane, upsetting passages got too close to earshot, Ramona turned the music up louder to drown them out.

In the morning, Ramona was the third to wake. Scarlett complained about the aftermath of their romp in Jägermeisterland and was packing up her stuff while Alice sat stone-like in the corner. Lenoir was presumably still in a deep slumber of eternal light or whatever new aged concept was hippest overseas but had yet to reach them in California.

Grasping her head, she felt the unforgiving grip of the hangover herself. She took two Tylenol's and offered the same to Scarlett.

"Ugh, that's the last time I let you talk me into Vitamin J again," she muttered.

"No one twisted your arm," Scarlett shot her a confronting look.

"Ooh, what crawled up your ass this morning?" Ramona fired back.

"My mom among other things. She's giving me shit for staying over so late."

"Christ, it's only—" she glanced over at the clock on the computer which trekked around the screen at a crawl. The last utterances of an ancient screensaver from an even more ancient computer system she had been begging her stepdad to update since the day he brought it home on clearance. "4:30? Wow, that's pretty damn late."

"Great party though, Rome. I didn't mean anything by it."

"Oh yeah, good times," she assumed she meant it sarcastically. "So where is sleeping beauty? Dreaming of the 'eternal light', I assume?"

Scarlett scoffs, "That or reading more passages from the book of the dead."

Ramona laughed too hard when the pounding headache reverberated within the walls of her head, sending shivers up her neck so painful it felt like her nervous system was on fire. She felt immensely guilty after the pain passed. After all, it was their friend sleeping in the guest bedroom that was the reason for the event in the first place. Now they were laughing at her, and what may be a more serious issue than either her or Scarlett wanted to acknowledge. This reminded her of Alice who sat awestruck on the floor of her den as if she'd been hypnotized and was waiting for someone to snap her out of her trance. "Alice, have you been up all night?"

Alice faced her, a dried bed of tears streaking her modest makeup and petite face. Her eyes were red and glassy, as if she were the one who had drank Jager all night. "I think something's really wrong with Noir."

Ramona rubbed her temples as if she were drowning from the hangover. She *didn't* need to have this conversation right now, but her guilt and dismissal of the issue, along with Alice's sad eyes won her over grudgingly. "You mean, besides the Kandarian demons she's summoning?"

Alice kept her face static, or she simply didn't understand the reference. "I think she might be under someone's influence, maybe this Isik guy she was talking about. I think she has brought others back with her too. When I was talking to her this morning, after you guys passed out, she mentioned 'others,' and referred to them as 'chaperones.' When I asked her to elaborate, she slyly changed the subject."

"She's a slippery bitch, that Lenoir Adams," Ramona agreed without a hint of mirth.

"So?" Alice pleaded with both her eyes and soul.

"So what?"

"So, if she's being brainwashed, don't you think we should tell someone? Or at least investigate further?"

"Who would we tell?"

"I don't know, Rome. I don't know," she was beginning to sound desperate and was getting on Ramona's last live nerve. "Her dad looked pretty upset about it. Maybe we could talk to him."

"So, you think Lenoir has been brainwashed and brought others back with her. Even if that were true, so

[58]

what? I thought when you commit someone, they have to be a danger to themselves or something?"

"I'm not joking around. You heard her last night. Does that sound like the Lenoir you know?"

"I don't know, Alice. I'm not really sure what you expect me to do here."

"I want you to first admit that something is definitely wrong. And then I want you to help me find out who is brainwashing her and why." Alice sounded firmer and more confident with each word.

"Would you stop saying brainwashed. Who do you think she is? Patty Hearst?" Ramona chuckled.

"More like John Walker Lindh." Alice folded her arms.

"Alice, I'm not sure what your hangup is," Ramona lied, "but I don't know what the hell you're talking about."

A fresh tear rolled down Alice's cheek, taking the same path as the old ones. "Yes, you do, you're just too afraid to do anything about it."

"What's going on?" a voice from across the room caused them both to jump.

Lenoir emerged with the same sweet and innocent smile on her face she always wore. However, there was a slight crimp in it this time, no doubt due to Alice's moaning.

"Oh nothing," Ramona waved a hand, "some people just don't realize that timing is everything," she glared at Alice.

"Aren't you going to say anything?" the ever-braver Alice scowled at Scarlett.

Scarlett looked uncomfortable, probably wishing she had already left. She held her head with one shoulder, surfing the next wave of pain before the Tylenol kicked in, and her overnight bag with her other. "Not really, I gotta go. My mom is all over my ass."

"What's wrong with the two of you?" Alice wailed, ready to lose her last ounce of sanity.

"Alice?" Lenoir's look of concern compounded. She took a step forward.

Frantic, Ramona bit her lip, trying to think of any way to avoid the conversation Alice seemed hell bent on having. She couldn't deal with it now. Not with the way the night went, she just needed to think on it. It was then she remembered. "Wait!"
Her friends looked at her with dismayed surprise, as if she just announced she was pregnant.

"Scarlett, you can't go yet. Not until we give her her present, remember?" Ramona beamed with pride that her brain could function on such little sleep and an oversaturation of Jag.

"Oh duh!" Scarlett smiled looking relieved as well. "Let's do it. Cause my mom is seriously ready to shit!"

"Are you sure that's what is going o-" Lenoir stuttered.

Ramona cut her off before Alice could confirm her doubts. "Of course, we meant to give it to you yesterday, but then everything got so silly."

Alice shook her head while Ramona dispensed a reassuring look that said *hold your fire* while her back was to Lenoir. She mouthed the words *later* in case there was any confusion before leaving to retrieve the gift bag.

"Yeah," Alice backpedaled rather skillfully considering her state a moment before. "We totally forgot about your gift. A sort of welcome home Noir thing," her voice shuddered.

Ramona appeared again a moment later and tossed a pink gift bag at Noir that was overflowing with red, sparkly tissue paper. "Welcome home babe," she added lamely.

"You guys didn't have to," she unhinged the taped handles and pulled it out, staring at it obtusely before her patented warm smile returned. "This will make my father really happy; he's been begging me to get one." She pulled out the plastic case it was housed in.

"Everybody has them now," Scarlet announced.

"Yeah, this way when we want to talk to you, we don't have to ask your dad or your sister to get you. That is sooo 20th century." Ramona quipped, feeling more and more relieved she was able to talk down Alice from her ledge.

Noir inspected the cellular phone closer, "What's the number?"

"It should be written on a card inside. It's called a 'TracFone,' so you add minutes when you run out. You should have five hundred to start with."

She looked at it, becoming more uninterested. "I don't know. On my trip I saw lots of people with these. They seem kind of intrusive."

"Once you get used to it, you'll never know how you got along without it," Alice added.

"Thanks you guys," Lenoir's smile unfolded as if it were a packed parachute. The corners and ends seemed to stretch out a mile wide. She moved forward to embrace them all in a group hug. "I still think we had the best rendition of *Waterfalls* that has ever been performed."

To which they all responded with a resounding full-throated laughter. It caused havoc on Ramona's head, but she held on to that feeling as if it were slipping away in a heavy gust of wind. She was suddenly struck with sadness by what had transpired before Noir awoke. It was then she realized why she was avoiding the difficult conversation Alice almost forced her to have. It was true, there was something wrong with Lenoir.

Part 4

A Light in the Black

So where are you?

You've depressed deeper into your dark abyss. This is the blackest part of your journey, the part where you could be lost in the flurry of the gloomier currents beneath you. You are dismayed from the light you've extended and the extent to which it has been rescinded. It's a swollen evening. A grandiose holiday filled with roadblocks and obscurities. They react with such glee and fortitude that they don't even see that they've lost the feeling to be free. These are the times you wonder about the world-- about what could have been-- about what could still be. You might even have the inclination to ignore your duty, if only for one cycle, but your rationale won't let you.

You look around to see the joy of your brothers and sisters, as if it were Maakan. But this place is no place at all without the light to guide them out. You glance at every fifth person who passes. The first attempts to guide you with bursts of light but fails to ignite you the way Isik has. The next is a self-goaded damsel that would be better off helping herself than waiting to be saved. They all want to be saved. They just can't see their crisis. There isn't enough light.

In the midst of this small fortress of corruption, always remember, you will lead them out. When you are high upon the hill, looking straight at the underbelly of their distracting structures, you will implore for them. You will ask forgiveness for them, whilst forgiving them. In the time that follows your selfless suffering, when you are basking in the light of Svarga kē rājya, they *will* repent you in infamy.

You know this time is difficult and it has you soaring lower than you've earned, but you may be able to carry them, if they can see the light. You can't help but wonder what it would be like to connect them with it, to connect with them again. But mind what they told you, your humanity will wilt away into something more beautiful, more evolved. They will always be part of you, you just have to let them go to let them in.

The pain is temporary.

Always remember your imminent contribution; the true gift of this season. Not one of bells, whistles or brightly colored paper that distract more than they inspire. Remember that your gift will go unnoticed at first, but you will be in your Makaan. You *will* be with the Giver of Light. Isik has amazing and beautiful things in store for you. The light shines on all your brothers and sisters that have accompanied you, but it will shine on you the brightest. Remember what he told you, not what they tell you now. If you can look past the fading facade of corruption that flows through them, poisoning their light, you will receive the greatest gift of all. Better than your ticket to California or your ticket back to Vaada Bhoomi. If you can forgive the transgressions of your past and accept your fate of the future, you will receive the greatest ticket of all.

Your ticket home.

"Alice? More lentils?" her father asked, smacking his lips.

Before she could answer, he dug into the container of take-out Indian they had ordered and heaped another helping onto his plate.

She watched him lackadaisically savoring the vegetables before sucking them down all the way. She glanced down to her own plate which had a few measly bites missing before pushing it away. He stopped chewing momentarily before looking up. "What is it dearie?" he asked in that grandfatherly way she hated. It always reminded her that he was old enough to be her grandfather, a fact she had always been embarrassed by growing up. They never discussed Alice's direct lineage very often, but she hated the fact she was the product of an old man's tryst with a young woman who soon realized her mistake and was never heard from again.

"Is it the clinicals?" he asked earnestly. "You know you are brilliant and that you needn't worry about such things."

She shook her head slowly, letting the gravity of the evening ahead weigh her down. "It's not the clinicals. It's—"

He was already on his next bite before he realized she stopped.

"Can you tell me about Uncle Chhaya?"

"Again?"

She nodded.

He sighed, probably not because he didn't like talking about his deceased brother, but more likely because he would have to stop eating the lentils. "You know the story, of course. He was killed in Khmer Rouge in '74. He stole all our meager possessions and gave them to the regime who attempted to have all of us killed. I escaped to Thailand where I worked as a sailor, until I came to California. You know the rest."

[65]

He had his fork poised, waiting to see if that satisfied her curiosity, which of course it never did. "When he came back, before he stole everything, what was he like? When the regime still had a hold on him?"

"Oh," her father said more gravely. He laid down his utensil, a look on his face appeared that said he too was no longer hungry. "He was not the same person. When someone's mind is ensnared, they really never are anymore. Even if you can bring them back, a piece of them was handed over to their captor, never to be heard from again. When I tried to talk sense into my brother, he heard me, but he never *heard* me. He was gone, all the parts with allegiance to us were. He jabbered on about communism and how it would save us all. He told us how we were living in sin with our glutinous ways. Glutinous! Us? My mother had to sell what he didn't steal to feed us scraps. I knew he put all his hopes in a lie, which is why I knew when he walked out that door the last time, that he was as good as dead. It was never confirmed, but I knew then, and I know now. So many died during that storm."

"Why didn't you try to save him?"

Her father groaned and something like a monster barked in his throat before he went on, "I tried—for a while. Their grip on him was too tight. Keep in mind my brother was much older than me, and he was also much smarter. If they were able to take such an intelligent mind with such ease and fortitude. What chance did I stand?" a wayward look in his eye grew.

"Wasn't it hard to let him go? Just like that."

He shook his head, his eyes were closed, but trembling. He was having trouble coming up with the words that would make her understand. "Not just like that. He was my brother. I tried in earnest for a very long time. I- I couldn't reach him. No one could. No one but the minister himself."

She was silent a time before she asked her next question. He seemed to stare at the lentils on his plate but may have been looking right through them. "Do you think there is anything you could have done or said that would have changed his mind?"

"No," he said more cheerily. "I suppose I could have clubbed him over the head and thrown him in a gunny sack."

Alice produced a chuckle. It hurt her lips and face to crease them so much.

"But at the time, I figured he was too smart to save. I think I was right."

Alice considered this, "My friend Lenoir. She's pretty smart."

"Ah yes, the well-travelled Lenoir! Will she be accompanying you tonight?"

"I hope so," Alice muttered, taking in this new information and trying to figure a way to apply it to her good friend's predicament.

Club Palace was where they had decided to ring in the new year. It was the Jägermeister twins' idea, of course. Scarlett and Ramona had pinched and saved and somehow convinced Alice to contribute toward a private room, which they had somehow managed to get on one of the busiest nights of the year. Alice was the last to arrive. On her way downtown she had stopped by a bookstore. It was not an intended stop, but she found herself gravitating to the self-help section and on a whim picked up a book entitled "Exit Strategy."

While her friends were likely getting situated in the private room and ordering the first round of drinks, she sat in the lot adjacent to the Palace and thumbed through her newest shelf ornament (which was what her father called books). She was determined to hatch a strategy to help Lenoir, or at least break through her impenetrable façade.

They had decided it was to be the four of them only for New Year's. Only Scarlett, the true social butterfly of the group had protested, but the spirit of their renewed bond had won her over. Alice couldn't view this as yet another reunion in the name of Lenoir being back. Instead, she it as a battlefield, and winning meant bringing back her friend. She surmised that the Jägermeister twins were simply still attempting to recapture the magic they had in high school.

The future keeps moving forward, Alice thought. *It is as impossible to stop as a moving train or coagulation of the blood after death.*

She decided that her battle plan would involve direct and forced communication if necessary. In the fifteen or so minutes of thumbing through *Exit Strategy* in the car, she came up with a list of questions to ask Lenoir in an attempt to show her how she had been manipulated. No easy feat. So, when she lifted back the velvet curtains that encased their private room, which turned out to be more of a private booth near the restrooms, Alice was dismayed to see that Lenoir had accessorized with dejection this evening. Not exactly a characteristic that forced communication.

"It's about time!" Ramona greeted her with a hug. It was an odd response considering Ramona had been avoiding Alice's calls like the plague after the sleepover. All Alice had needed was a sounding board, someone to bounce an idea off.

"Great music tonight!" Scarlett's eyes scanned the booth as if she could see through the curtains and into the club.

"You know the four of us are going to kill it out on the dance floor later? Once we get our liquid courage on," Ramona nodded.

"Do you know who this is?" Scarlett screamed over a set of bass thumps that threatened to level the building. "It's Scotty Janacek. Do you remember him? He was a grade ahead of us I think."

[68]

No one seemed to know, or maybe they all had more pressing things on their mind. Alice sensed something was off with Ramona and Noir and part of her wished she hadn't been so absorbed in *Exit Strategy* and had come in sooner.

"I think he calls himself DJ Scotty J now," Scarlett finished the thought.

"That sounds real original," Ramona scoffed.

"So why does everyone look like they just came back from a funeral?" Scarlett sounded defensive. Perhaps she had a thing for Mr. DJ Scotty J.

"I think we're in mourning. We are mourning 2001. What a strange and wonderful year it was," Lenoir swirled her wine glass.

"It was a shit year!" Ramona shouted over more bass. "I'm ready to turn the page. Bring on 2002!"

"Hear hear, girl!" Scarlett cheered as they clinked glasses.
Lenoir smiled, watching them happily recount the moments that led them up to the present.

The server poked her head in from behind the red velvet curtain, "How are we doing in here ladies?"

The Jägermeister twins cheered as if it were almost midnight and the ball was ready to drop.

The server noticed Alice and asked if she wanted anything.

"Chardonnay," Alice said after deciding it would be easier to pretend to drink than explain to the others why she had no interest.
"I'll be right back with that," the server's teeth looked like ivory bones sticking out of red clay.

As she went to retrieve Alice's wine, the curtain was left open, allowing the swirling lighting display outside to tumble in and perform calisthenics around them. It wasn't too long before a group of guys in their thirties used the opening as their own personal shopping window. "Hey ladies," one with a bow tie and his hair spiked up drooled. "Can we buy you a round?"

"Easy boys," Scarlett handled them with ease. "'Ladies' don't like it when you're overeager. Catch us out on the dancefloor in an hour. We're talking right now."

"Ya'll are good friends, huh?" a short one behind the bow-tied man piped in.

"You must be the clever one," Ramona retorted. "Come on dudes, move along. You're sucking up our oxygen."

"Save a dance for me," the bow-tied one took Ramona's quip as a compliment and winked.

They closed the curtain primly, but it was opened back up once the server returned with Alice's drink and— surprise—four shot glasses filled with some unknown hyper-alcoholic merger. "Anything else right now?" the server asked once everyone had a shot in front of them.

"Please," Scarlett winked at all of them. "Could you try and keep the fans away? We rented a private room for privacy."

The server took a step back and eyed them all suspiciously until she had her *Eureka* moment. "Of course," her mouth stretched open to reveal a smile. "I had no idea it was *you!*"

They all glanced at one another, amused.

"Not me, you goof. It's her," she thumbed sideways, pointing at Lenoir who sat up slightly embarrassed.

The server looked Lenoir up and down and while her smiled faded slightly, "Of course, my apologies."

"You know of the Lost Lenoir, right?" Scarlett continued.

"Who doesn't?!" the server squealed. "I will make sure our head of security is informed and please let us know if anyone else bothers you. We want you to enjoy your evening. Are you sure I can't bring you something else? A bottle of champagne maybe?"

[70]

"Have one at the ready around five to midnight," Scarlett answered.

"Absolutely, consider it done," the server flashed more admiration toward Lenoir before she left.

They all had a good laugh.

"Could her nose get any browner?" Ramona tried to hold her composure.

"Maybe she saw us up on stage performing Waterfalls," the knot in Alice's stomach had loosened as she forgot to *not* drink the chardonnay that was delivered.

"I'm telling you, this new book I'm reading by this guy Stafford is crazy. Lesson number one, if you say anything confidently enough, people will buy it. Arm yourselves," Scarlett raised her shot glass inviting the rest to follow.

They clinked and downed what turned out to be kamikazes. Alice grimaced at the flavor and the wretched aftertaste.

"Actually, the more confidence you show outwards the more your internal light extinguishes. Only false prophets mistake arrogance with confidence. Fooling man is not a victory, it is a folly. Isik Veren told me that on my last night."

"Boy the guest of honor is full of wisdom tonight," Ramona droned.

"Poor lost Lenoir," Scarlett added.

"Not all those who wander are lost," Lenoir reminded them.

"Quoth the raven—" Ramona stuck her tongue out.

"Are you going to make that stupid joke every time we get together?" Scarlett asked her.

"Maybe you should put down Stafford and pick up Poe."

"Hmm," Scarlett thought on it, "Is he hot?"

"Maybe we should raise another glass. This time to friendship," Alice tried her best to keep the peace while Ramona and Scarlett exchanged stink eyes.

It seemed to silence the bickering at least.

"I think I'm going to go hit the floor. I'm feeling good and I think bow tie man has it bad for yours truly. Anyone coming?" Scarlett asked.

"We'll catch up. I need to finish my courage first," Alice indicated her half glass of wine.

"Ramona?"

"Sure," she lifted the curtain, "maybe you can get me Scotty DJ's autograph."

"You know no one can say 'no' to us," Scarlett outstretched a hand which Ramona took, concluding their spat– if that's what it was.

They left the curtain open, and just before Alice pulled it shut to discourage more interruptions, Scarlett stuck her head back in. "Try not to bring each other further down the spiral while we're gone, k guys?" Scarlett blew them a kiss and closed the curtain tight.

Once it was clear they were gone for good, Alice shook her head, "Those two."

"They haven't changed all that much, have they?" Lenoir noted.

"I guess not. This is the most I've seen them in a long while."

"Have you been trying to escape them?"

"No, of course not. They are our friends."

"But it seems like you've changed. You seem a lot more serious than you used to be."

"I suppose I have, but it seems like everyone's going through changes right now. Busy time in life and all that." Alice took this opportunity to start working her the way *Exit Strategy* compelled. Can I ask you a question?"

"Of course," Lenoir inched herself closer to Alice in the U-shaped booth.

[72]

"What's been the biggest change in your life now compared to before you left?"

Lenoir's smile grew substantially, "Easy, the light has changed me."

"In what way?"

"In every way possible."

"Okay, what is the light making you feel right now?" Alice proceeded.

"Right now?" Lenoir thought, "Right now it is making me feel a bit of sadness."

"And you don't think that's just the holiday blues. A lot of people feel that this time of year. It's a psychological reaction to extreme highs. For instance, seeing people you haven't seen in a while, the mad rush of the holiday season and then the inevitable free fall when it's over. It can leave you feeling empty. Maybe not for Ramona and Scarlett since they've stuck around. It's like a mountain bike, we are all in different gears. You are in the first gear, the widest chain because you're the most traveled, so you face the biggest drop-off. It's like you're pedaling so hard just to keep the endurance going. They're sustaining themselves in the same old gear they've always been in. They've never had to change. I'm somewhere in between, I suppose. My point is everyone feels like that. Even those who haven't been introduced to the light. In fact, it may have nothing to do with the light at all. Couldn't that be true?"

"I know what you're trying to do, Alice. Unfortunately, my sadness is not as simple as that. Everything has to do with the light. The light is given to every man, woman and child. Once they accept the light's power, it fills them in a way that they could never ignore it again."

"What if the light is a disguise for something else? What if it was designed as something to fool and harm? What if something malicious is underneath the light?"

[73]

"You make it sound like Science Fiction, Alice. It is a very real, very simple thing in its purest form. And that's the beauty of any light; nothing can escape its luminosity. Therefore, nothing can hide underneath it because it illuminates everything and is transparent. There is not a thing that can use it as a cloak because light is the complete antithesis of that."

"Have you ever heard of a black hole? A force so powerful it swallows up everything in its path-- even light."

"What you're talking about is darkness, Alice. And darkness can be anywhere. That is the real cloak and dagger scheme. This, outside this booth, out on the dancefloor, outside this building, in the parking lot, everywhere. That is the real camouflage, the real darkness. I know you can see it too. I may come on a little strong, but I know you are different. I know we are really talking about the same thing. For me, it has just come fully into focus. I wish I could make you see that. I wish I could make *them* see that. That is the darkness that eats away at me. That is what has brought on my sadness. I know they said it wouldn't be easy, but I never thought it would be this difficult."

In a certain way, Alice agreed with her. As a new song came erupting out of the sound system inside Club Palace, Alice stayed silent, thinking about what to say next. She panicked at the thought of her plan going awry, but that was just what it seemed to be doing. It was exactly what her father had said about his brother, he was too smart. Lenoir was smart as well, and she seemed to fully embrace the pull of whatever was inside her. She embraced it so much that Alice could almost sense it pulling on her as well.

They listened to the music for a time, a pulsing beat with an atmospheric build up and a robotic voice that was a little hard to understand. It was saying something about the power of dance, which seemed to be on par with most of the electronic music Alice had heard before. Some kind of organ, electronic piano and more rhythms joined halfway through until the voice came back again, instructing those who listened to dance until they dropped dead, which to Alice seemed like terrible advice, but status quo for a dance club.

"So, if the light is everything to you? How do you have room for anything else? Do you not still value friends, family, security, success? All those things?" Alice finally asked.

"The light touches everything, including those things. Therefore, the light is everything."

"What about purpose?"

"My main purpose now is to draw others to the light."

Alice *was* panicking, this was not how she wanted it to go at all. To combat this awful, berating and downright suffocating feeling, she swigged the rest of her wine in several loud gulps that seemed to mirror the beat of the music.

As if she were standing right outside, waiting for her cue, the server poked her head back in and asked if they needed anything else. Alice tried to repeat her order from before, but due to the music, all she could do was point to her empty glass and the server seemed to understand. But not before taking another extended glance at Lenoir, who would forever be a star to her due to Scarlett's lame joke. Alice felt like crying as she gazed at Lenoir. Lenoir returned her a sweet, innocent smile that said she could read her mind and was okay with what she was attempting to do. It showed she cared. Because of this transparency, Alice never had felt more inferior.

She took one last stab, "So what makes you so certain? How can you be one hundred percent on this light? How can you be one hundred percent on what this Isik is saying to you? How do you know you are not being used?"

Lenoir took her friend's shaking hand into hers, "You know as well as I do that nothing is for certain in this life,

[75]

Alice. Our faith and belief are what makes us special. You only know because the feeling tells you."

"How do you know when it tells you?"

"Easy, you listen for it. It's like being in love for the first time. You just know. You can hear it; you can feel it."

"Then it *is* like what we talked about at Ramona's. You're in love."

"Very much indeed. And you know what it is like when you're in love? You want to spread that love around. You want to make everyone see what you see. That way everyone you care about is as happy and ecstatic as you are, knowing this love, this truth. That's what love is. And that's what light is."

"So, if someone were to say to you that your love and light is complete bullshit, what would you tell them?"

"I wouldn't say anything. I'd try my best to cast the light on them and I'd move on. Not everyone can be made to see the light, not everyone is ready to feel it," she squeezed Alice's hand tighter. "But you are. You need it now more than ever."

She let go and Alice swallowed hard to suppress her tears. It felt like she was almost ready to go along with whatever Lenoir told her. She felt it calling to her just like the black hole she described before. She felt the influence of the hold that was on her friend deeply. It rendered her helpless, brainless and powerless all at once. If it weren't for the hypnotic catcalls and cheers coming from outside the booth, along with the chants of *Dance until you drop dead*, Alice would have been completely swallowed up by the movement that had swallowed Lenoir. She was sure of it. She wondered why here—at Club Palace of all places. Why hadn't she been completely consumed a few weeks prior in the steely silence of Ramona's den? Was it because she was so emotionally invested now? Or was this the first real and honest conversation she had had since Lenoir had come back? Also, why hadn't Lenoir come in for the kill? Why did she let her dangle there? Did Lenoir sense that Alice's was not quite ready after all and then backed off?

Before she found her answer, Lenoir swung around to the other side of the booth, stood up and parted the curtains. "I have to run to the lady's room. If she comes back, order me a dry martini, will you?" She flashed a smile and went on her way, leaving Alice with the desperate, desolating feeling of her failure. It highlighted how ill equipped she was to take on whatever had entranced the happy and willful girl she once knew in high school.

The server came back, and Alice ordered Lenoir's drink, but it was a blur. The alcohol had not gotten to her, it was more the debilitating feeling like getting run over by a bulldozer. Defeated, she removed herself from their booth and wandered out into the club. She drifted in and out of the other booths, some of the curtains left open, allowing the drunken depravity inside to leak out. As Alice moved closer to the main room, the lights blinked on and off and moved at bewildering speeds. It seemed to slow down time. Alice was beaten, but not broken. After all this relaxed measure of time allowed an equally short-schemed plan to form in her head as she moved past the boys with stars in their eyes and the pixies they had set their sights on. They moved rhythmically in tight circles, like they were searching for items that had fallen from their pockets. Only the pockets didn't have holes in them and so they would be forced to perform this movement forever. She moved past eyes that defamed and looked unscrupulously at parts she was not yet comfortable with. She ignored the mindless one-liners that came from the greasy haired lechers who uttered them. Past them, there, in the middle of the floor she found the Jägermeister twins dancing together. Scarlett swayed stiffly while Ramona marched to the beat of the drum machine gushing out of the speakers above them. Bubbles and confetti dropped from somewhere above as if the equilibrium wasn't out of balance enough.

The hot, sweaty residue seemed to solidify in midair as bodies of mass bumped into Alice and moved to a beat that was constantly shape shifting. She watched them perform this embarrassing ritual for a couple of measures before she locked onto Ramona. After all, it was a couple weeks previous that Ramona had showed the most promise in unmasking whatever it was that infected Lenoir. Perhaps she was the key to unraveling the tightly rolled knot that had slid around her stomach like a boulder on ice.

Alice thought of her father and his attempts to pry his brother from the Khmer Rouge and realized she had to try. What kind of doctor would she turn out to be if she turned tail and ran at the first sight of blood? She supposed, not a very good one.

Scarlett caught sight of her and squealed. She chirped something unintelligible to which Alice nodded and joined Ramona in the circle. Another ditty came cascading through the speakers. It was a tune that spoke of love and the power of its influence as an electronic melodic organ promised to bring those on the dance floor even higher than they already were. Scarlett seemed to take the bait. She tilted her head back and closed her eyes as she danced. As Alice psyched herself up next to Ramona, she noticed Scarlett leaning further back and her glass full of melting ice sliding out of her hand. Before she could reach in, a man's hand came into the picture and effortlessly caught it just as it was about to fall from her fingertips. At the same time, he caught Scarlett before she would have fallen completely backwards. She neither seemed startled or expectant of this action. Still not opening her eyes, she nuzzled her head into the slender, well-dressed man's chest as he pulled her closer.

"Guess it's just me and you, babe" Ramona, not quite as drunk, crooned into Alice's ear as she wrapped her arms around her shoulders. The tight, unexpected grip momentarily caught Alice off guard, but she supposed certain accommodations would have to be made if she were going to enlist Ramona's help.

"Does she know that guy?" Alice motioned with her head toward the man who held Scarlett.

Ramona shrugged, "I think he's a friend of that clever one from before."

"The bow-tie man?!" she shouted over the music.

Ramona nodded slowly, leaning back herself, forcing Alice to lead as she twirled with more grace than she usually carried.

"Can I talk to you for a moment?" she bit her lip.

"If you can dance, you can talk," Ramona explained.

"It's important."

"Is it about our bubbly? It's still coming at midnight, right?

"Not that."

Ramona used Alice's hand to pull herself up so that they were face to face while the lack of choreography continued. "What sort of wonderland has Alice stumbled into this time?"

"It's about Lenoir," she tried to mask her grief.

Ramona's eyes rolled and suddenly the feisty girl she'd always known had come back, which relieved her. If she was going to have any chance of battling Lenoir's strong-willed demons, she would need that potency on her side. "Please Alice, not tonight. It's New Years."

"If not tonight, when?"

Ramona uttered one of her world-famous huffs. The music drowned out the sound, but Alice felt its cool wind. What she failed to feel was that a tight circle of onlookers was forming around them. They encouraged the girls to dance closer, as more carnal suggestions followed. Writhing in her own discomfort, Alice was able to smile at them, which seemed to amuse Ramona.

"Tell you what," Rome gushed, "Help me give them a show and we can talk about any little thing your heart desires."

"She had me," Alice warned. "She had me dead to rights, just as certain as they have her now."

They twisted along with the music, and then Ramona took charge and pulled Alice in by the waist, much to the delight of the salivating men crowded around them.

"They who, Alice? You're starting to sound like a crazy old cat lady."

"The same thing happened to my uncle, he joined a cult and eventually he was never heard from again."

"And you think the same thing is going to happen to Noir?"

"Yes!"

More hoots and hollers followed as the men took Alice's agreement as some kind of lustful declaration. Bemused, Ramona smacked her on the ass as the melody shifted again—this time into a more soulful track that invigorated the dancers and forced them to dial it up a notch.

"What are you doing?" Alice asked.

"I'm giving them a show," Ramona eyed the bow tied man who had shown her interest earlier.

Then it was Alice's turn to grab Ramona's shoulders. She found it hard to concentrate while performing this ridiculous charade, but it was the only way she could get her recruit to listen. Playing along, she dipped Ramona and they circled one another with their arms outstretched as if they were dancing a tango.

Suddenly, chants of *kiss kiss kiss* erupted from the crowd. Alice rolled her eyes both at the attention their dance was gaining, and Ramona's insistence of the performance while shooting suggestive looks at the bow tied man. With her frustrations boiling and her patience wearing thin, she grabbed Ramona by the shoulders again and

[80]

shook her harder than she intended. The bystanders only took it as another part of the sultry dance in which the two were entangled. More lewd remarks rang out, hardly audible over the music. Comments such as *Oh yeah, rough stuff* and *Friends with benefits* were fired scattershot one after the other.

However, Ramona could still tell the difference, "Whoa, take it easy! I need that shoulder to play softball this spring."

"I need you to listen to me, Ramona. I mean really listen to me!" Alice felt her mask slipping. "I need your help because I can't do what I need to do alone," she gritted her teeth and tried to remain upbeat as the stares from the men around them grew more confused. They were beginning to see that this was no romp or fair-weather flirtation, Alice was deadly serious.

"Look, I can't help you with Lenoir!"

"Why not?!"

"Because there is nothing TO HELP!"

Alice stared at her a moment, trying to pierce her stubborn nature. Trying to determine her next course in an evening where revamping one's plans was becoming commonplace.

"Fine, it's because I can't help," Rome admitted during a quieter interlude of the song.

"Of course you can. You are the most hardheaded of us all and if anyone can make Lenoir listen, I have to believe it's you."

To her complete surprise, Ramona's face transformed before her eyes. Her chin quivered and her face turned a darker shade of red under the woozy lights. Some waterworks came out, but Ramona practically pinched herself to push them back. The only benefit of this new revelation was that the hormonally challenged group quickly lost interest and retreated to the bar for drinks. "I don't know why you have to do this nooow!" Ramona complained.

"We're losing her," Alice pointed toward the back of the Club Palace, toward their private booth. "Why is this so hard for you to understand?"

Strangely, Ramona pulled Alice close to her in an embrace, but it was no longer for the benefit of the patrons of Club Palace. Alice felt her need to unburden as she shook within her grasp. A couple of the leftover fanboys remained, and their interest piqued momentarily. "You know about my dad, don't you Alice?" she mouthed the words but the fraught sound that came out seemed to be a complete mismatch.

Alice shook her head, "Yeah, too cheap to buy a modern computer, what about him?"

Ramona giggled nervously, wiping her nose with the back of her hand. Alice thought she looked like a little kid. "No, that's my stepdad," she said nasally. "I mean my real dad. My *dad dad*."

Alice shook her head again.

Ramona's hands were on Alice's hips as they danced middle school style in slow, wayward semi circles to music that required double or even triple the speed. But it was no longer about the dance or the music or the perverse delight of those that surrounded them. It was about two friends having a conversation that was already tardy in Alice's mind. "Well, my dad was an alcoholic. It didn't happen so long ago that I don't remember. Maybe most days I like to forget, actually."

"I thought he got a job on the other side of the country."

Ramona smiled emphatically as more tears squeezed past her guard.

It seemed that Alice had struck a nerve, more collateral damage she hadn't anticipated or realized until it was too late. Earlier in the evening she had accidently tore open the old wounds of her own father, now she was stomping all over the very placid, and who knew it, fragile memories, of her good friend Ramona.

"I guess that is not totally inaccurate," another series of breathy giggles escaped her like spent oxygen from a balloon. "He got a job in the laundry. But he was an alcoholic who never knew when to give up his keys. He drove drunk thousands of times. My mom only could take so much. But one night he drove again, plastered, after a Monday football game with his buddies. That was the night he never came home. I was young, but I remembered. His prior convictions fucked him over awfully. He was sent to Federal prison. Criminal Vehicular Homicide, I think they call it. Anyway, I remember the time between when it happened and when he was going away. I didn't understand. My mom was being a bitch for all I knew. She wouldn't forgive him. She kept telling me, 'He doesn't want our help, Mona.' I couldn't believe that." Her eyes opened wider, and she stood straight up.

"My dad told me when I was little that everyone was worth helping. Even back then, I thought that was some kind of coded message that he was trying to tell me. Anyway, he moved to an apartment just down the road from us. He wasn't giving up trying to see us, and we spent a lot of time together the weekends before he left. I didn't realize it at the time, but he lost his job, so after that we started seeing him even more on the weeknights too. It was summer. One day, on a day I wasn't scheduled to see him, I biked down the street to his apartment. I looked up in the window and saw his light on. I knocked on his door and he answered, drunk, of course. Even as he was awaiting prison, he was still swilling' it down like there was no tomorrow.

"But I was used to seeing him that way. I forced my way in after he tried to get me to leave. I tried to talk to him. I tried to save him. But you know what? My mom

[83]

was right," she wiped at her eyes again. "He didn't want to be saved. As I sat on his dingy furniture in his den, he just sat there with this extinct look on his face. He looked like he was lost at sea with no hope of finding life and not giving two shits about it. I'll never forget that look. After I was done crying my eyes out, he just told me to go home. There was this huge fakeness on his face. Even his actions, it's like he was just going through the motions, like he knew something better was awaiting him once he was done. I never would have recognized at the time. It's like, he always acted like a father rather than being one. He always acted like he knew what was best for me but then wouldn't practice it himself. It was so- so- fucking phony!" she shook her head, seeming almost intolerant of the idea. "I'll never forget that look in his eyes," she repeated, "I've never even thought about forgiving it either. That's why I don't visit him out in Lewisburg either."

Ramona paused and stared deep into Alice's eyes, "You're probably wondering why I'm telling you this story. What it has anything to do with Noir."

"The eyes," Alice croaked.

Ramona stared for another moment, her large, dark brown eyes themselves looked completely hopeless. The very antithesis of what she preached earlier about the New Year and all the optimism. Then her face contorted and shrank back into the look that Alice only supposed she wore on her face the day she said goodbye to her *dad dad*. It was in the eyes. That fake plastic smile can appear on anyone's face, but the eyes will not lie. Alice's own father had brought home this point to her on many occasions.

"Lenoir has had those same eyes ever since she's been back," Ramona vocalized what they were both thinking. "I can't go through that again. I'm sorry," Ramona whimpered and pulled away from Alice. Her eyes darted around Club Palace like she was looking for a place to throw up, but her mind wasn't able to make a decision.

[84]

"I can't," she threw the words at Alice before running away. She ran back through the dancers that began to grow again once a new, uplifting tune started.

Alice remained on the dance floor for another minute, collecting her thoughts. Wishing she hadn't dug up the old wounds of her friend now, especially since it didn't lead her to lend the hand she thought she would. She also thought about Ramona herself. How guarded she had been in the past in making Alice think she was something she wasn't. And now, Lenoir herself. She had also been pretending to be something she wasn't: a strong-willed woman who was completely independent and confident. Unless the persona she'd worn since she had been back was the fake. Between the wine, the emotional evening and the absent mindedness in being unable to feed herself much of a dinner, the room began to spin around Alice, lapping her at every corner, running her over at every straight away.

The pulsing music and declining gravity was too much to handle, and soon Alice found herself making a B-line in the same manner Ramona did. She ran for the bathroom and made it well enough. For the rest of the hour, the two of them sat side by side in the stalls, ignoring one another's pain. Ignoring their own pain. Wanting desperately to end a hurtful, gut wrenching New Year's evening while still pretending everything was okay.

Later, in another corner of Club Palace, Lenoir emerged from wherever she hid and joined the rest of them out on the dancefloor. By then Alice had been feeling much better and was slowly working on another glass of wine. Scarlett busied herself with a guy in the corner. They were talking, laughing, kissing and taking shots of some kind of clear spirit. Once Alice noticed her at the end of the bar, she wondered to herself if it was the same guy she was talking to earlier. The evening had been a blur. She wasn't even sure where her purse was and whether anyone had been back to their private booth to check.

Once Lenoir emerged from the shadows, her face beamed with the light she had so exhaustively searched for in her travels. The house music picked up another beat, and the floor was filled to the brim with sweaty bodies, foul breath and warm thoughts of what's to come. It was a strange atmosphere. As she floated out onto the dancefloor, she had a look of pure unadulterated pleasure on her face. Even Scarlett took notice because when Lenoir graced Alice's side, she asked, "Did you just have sex in the bathroom?"

Lenoir, not the slightest bit embarrassed of the question or even the thought answered, "What I have is better than any piece of ass."

Scarlett laughed strangely, not quite understanding, "If you say so. I'm glad you are finally out here. Now!" She pointed up toward the DJ booth. Alice squinted through the lights circling the glib darkness and saw another hand wave back. It was Ramona, hanging all over the DJ who's name she had deemed so uncreative hours earlier.

The music quieted and the lights came up brighter. DJ Scotty J boomed over the music like his was the voice of God with a very important message. "I want to give a Club Palace shout out to the Long-Lost Lenoir who has just returned from abroad. She's a wicked world traveler who has just returned and is joining us tonight to ring in the New Year. Welcome back to the world, LENOIR! Love, everyone who truly knows you!" he read the message distinctly enough, if not a little bit dispassionately.

"What's going on?" Lenoir, unfazed by this onslaught of sudden attention, asked.

"You're getting your shout out!" Scarlett, discarding her latest gentleman friend, pulled Noir out onto the floor and the two of them put on an energetic medley of all the dance moves they had ever picked up. They were killing it

[86]

too. But after a while the circle that formed around them closed and everyone joined. Alice danced with half the energy she had before. Ramona eventually reunited with them on the floor. She seemed to have forgot about the excruciating discussion that had occurred earlier.

Alice didn't even remember the change to New Year's. She remembered the champagne and inane dialog with a group of cute guys who claimed they were in law school. But the grand countdown to the evening had already come and gone, lost in that blur once again. Since no more of her objectives were likely to be completed, it seemed entirely appropriate to lose herself in the music and the night. She lost herself with Lenoir too. The two had danced for hours together-- maybe days even, perhaps eons.

Once the house lights came up for good and less than a hundred people remained in the club, the girls stumbled back to their private booth to check on their belongings. Ramona crept up behind Alice and sloppily draped her arms over her shoulders, giving her a fright as she wound up to punch what was sure to be a third string pervert trying to make his move. "What a night, eh?"

Alice nodded, holding her head. She removed a compact from her purse to make sure she didn't look as horrible as she felt. "A night for the ages," she whispered to no one in particular.

"A night for the ages," Rome repeated with a giggle. "I like that."

"Too many cute guys to pick from so I guess I will have a new line of prospects this year," she slurred. "I wonder if any of them called me yet."

"How many did you give your number to?"

"How's am I supposed to know?" she burped and tried to cover her mouth too late.

"Do yourself a favor and don't count," Scarlett had also crept up behind Alice but gave her less of a scare.

"Jesus, you guys!" Alice gave her a playful shove.

[87]

"I see that 2001's Alice decided to stayover for 2002," Scarlett chided her.

"You don't seem too tipsy," She ignored her, "Are you driving home?"

"I didn't drive here; I took a cab. I'm getting a ride from him," she pointed behind them.

There stood what Alice could only determine to be the third semi-serious prospect of the evening. Scarlett certainly had a type! This guy too was tall, not quite as slender, but more on the muscular side, and dark skinned.

"You sure?" Alice asked, not as concerned as she led on.

"Oh yeah! Boy has a Vette, what am I supposed to say, no?"

"Who you callin' 'boy'?" he laughed.

After Alice dug through her purse for some mascara to reapply, she gave up. Maybe it wasn't her job to protect them, Scarlett or Lenoir. Maybe Rome was right. Maybe they didn't want to be saved. Then her mind drifted to logistics. She wondered how the other two were getting home. It was quite clear that even though she only had three glasses of wine, it would be ill advised to drive home. Besides, there were a whole mess of other beverages that had been shoved under her nose throughout the night, and she wasn't sure how many she had succumbed to.

Clearly not satisfied with Alice's reaction to her suitor, Scarlett continued to vie for their attention. "Isn't he dreamy? I think he looks like Cris Judd, minus the goatee of course."

"More like John Walker Lindh," Ramona noticed after gathering her coat, extra pair of shoes and purse in her hands and hugging them to her chest like they were a large stack of books.

Alice raised an eyebrow, watching Scarlett struggle to put a face to the name.

Eventually she gave up, asking "What show is he on?"

"Where's Noir?" Alice asked.

"She's talking to this dude in a white robe who thinks he's Jesus or something," Ramona muttered, holding one eye open and trying to read the display on her Nokia. "This thing should be coming alive right now," she slurred the words.

"You know what? I'd like to be doing the same thing in about an hour. How about we go rescue the lost girl from Jesus and get out of here? The staff looks like they are ready to bust a nut too," Scarlett coaxed.

After a semi-exhaustive search for Noir, plus a couple of detours to stop by the bathroom to hold Ramona's hair away from her face, they headed outside.

"Rome, let me use your phone to call a cab?" Alice decided to make an executive decision.

"I can call," she started hitting random buttons on her Nokia.

"You bitches are dense if you think you're getting a cab at this time of night. On New Years!" Scarlett petted her companion as they squeezed through the security team at the front of the club.

Ramona then placed the phone, upside down, under her chin to get a better grip on her purse. She dropped it as they exited the club. The phone fell to the sidewalk and shattered into an unimpressive five pieces. "Oh fizz!" she shrieked unintelligibly.

"Way to go you freakin' klutz," Scarlett and her stranger immediately bent over to pick up and pocket the pieces of cellular technology.

Ramona, vaguely unaware she even broke her prized possession began singing *Waterfalls* once again, as Scarlett joined her. When the four of them cemented their place on the sidewalk, Lenoir emerged behind them.

"Fucking in the bathroom, again?" Scarlett pretended to be angry.

"Sorry, was talking to a companion," Alice thought she detected a slight bit of frustration or hurt in her tone. But her copper toned, artificial smile beamed all the brighter when Alice scrutinized her with a long look.

"What champion?" Rome rested her head on Alice's shoulder. "Jesus?"

Tired of drunken friends, epic failures and other exploits, Alice sighed, allowing Ramona to recharge. At least her sudden inabilities would keep her quiet and in one place.

As Lenoir and Scarlett conversed about trivial things, Alice thought that wounded tone might allow one more attempt at heroics. Maybe this late at night, in all of their intoxicated states, maybe now was the best time to strike. As Alice struggled to balance Ramona, her purse, and the ridiculous shoes Scarlett insisted upon her borrowing for the evening, she interrupted their chatter, "You want to share a cab?"

"I already told you, Gump, I'm riding home with my boy here," Scarlett looked perplexed.

"I called us a cab," Lenoir stated disinterestedly.

"That's a relief," Alice removed a piece of Ramona's hair from her eyes. "One of you want to give me a hand with her?"

"Is she down for the count?" Scarlett asked, stepping in to remove some of the weight off Alice.

"It seems so."

"She's going to rage about her phone when she remembers."

"It's her own fault," Alice muttered.

As the chatter died down Lenoir stood lost in her own thoughts, more lost than when she was away for all those years, maybe even more lost than she looked in her whole life. She was the only object in a beam of light that seemed to stretch out and beyond her. It was as if her own precious light had tripped her up somehow, effortlessly casting her mortal fiber aside. She looked like a thin piece of fabric swaying on a clothesline. Then, out of nowhere, she asked, "Who do I owe for the bill inside?"

Alice and Scarlett glanced at one another, and then a sheepish grin came to Scarlett's face as she struggled with the extra weight in her arms.

Alice sighed. All she wanted to do was climb in the cab that was supposedly coming. She had cooked up a new angle in which to question Lenoir, and she was certain that she would not even see it coming. She stalked around for a moment, "I suppose we should see if we can settle the bill."

"A good idea," Lenoir nodded and turned to Scarlett. "You okay watching her?"

Scarlett rolled her eyes, "Yeah, but hurry your asses up. Your cab's still coming."

Lenoir smiled strangely, "We won't miss it."

They strolled up to the door where the bouncers made a point to move in front of it. "You left something inside, call the manager's office tomorrow. No one gets back in," one of them grumbled.

"We forgot to pay our bill," Alice protested.

He eyed her suspiciously, glancing over at Lenoir like the two of them were trying to con him out of something. "Call the manager's office tomorrow. Have a good night, ladies." He then turned to his partner and spoke loudly about the upcoming Orange Bowl game in January.

Scarlett sniggered at the sight of them back so soon as she handed Ramona off to Lenoir, who accepted her with an abnormal kind of physical prowess. "Are we off the hook?"

"What? Did you plan that?" Alice asked, slightly disturbed.

Scarlett grinned, "I wouldn't even know how to begin."

After what seemed like an eternity, their cab finally pulled up to the curb. While Scarlett helped Alice load Ramona's lifeless body into it, they noticed Lenoir had disappeared again. Then, right before she was to wonder aloud, she reappeared and casually swooped in to say her goodbyes to Scarlett.

"Where were you?" Alice asked her when the door shut and the goodbyes had been said.

"I was right here," Lenoir placed a hand on Alice's arm, not unkindly. "I've always been right here."

With Ramona slumped in one corner of the cab, and Lenoir's head now resting on her shoulder, Alice grew sweaty and restless. The physical weight, combined with the figurative was causing her to suffocate. After some talk radio that the driver kept turning up after asking directions, and back down after he was lost again, the miles drifted by in shadows only eclipsed by neon Christmas light fever dreams.

"Lenoir," Alice whispered to the relative stranger on her shoulder.

"Hmm," Lenoir groaned as if she were half asleep. Again, it sounded completely deceptive.

"Do you remember what it was exactly that you were looking for? After high school?"

Lenoir sat up slowly, like a zombie crawling out of its grave. Her cute up-do from earlier was now a tad disheveled near the temple, "What I was looking for?"

"Yeah," Alice replied, "You know. When you left after high school. When you went on your 'journey.'"

"Oh," she sat up tighter. She closed her eyes serenely and took a joyful deep breath. "I was looking for the light."

Alice felt something pop, like there was a break in some vital piece of her. She knew it was just anxiety, but it felt like something else, something heavier, something that could alter her own path in treacherous ways. "Well," she cleared her throat. "I'm glad you found it."

She looked out the window at the passing neighborhoods. Shadows of holiday trees and holly covered shrubs seemed to reach out to her. She would have gladly taken their offered limbs if she could. Anything was better than being in the cab right now. Her thoughts meandered back to her father. How hard it must have been to confront his only brother on such a desperate matter. This was a test.

"Anyone can find it you know. At any time. It is already inside of us; you just have to find the right way to let it out. When you do, it will shine down on you warmer than any embrace you've had, it will make you feel safer than a thousand bodyguards and more loved than all the family in the world."

"Sounds like it covers everything you would ever need," Alice kept her poker face.

"It's more than about that."

"Oh?"

"For me it is. I think it could be for you too."

"Why is the light different for you than it is for everyone else? I thought it was the same light."

Lenoir smiled, "Don't you see? It is the same light, but I'm different."

"A lot different than I remember."

"Alice," Lenoir hugged her, it felt clammy and empty. "We are not the same as everyone else, me and you."

"What do you mean by that?"

"Take a look around you," she outstretched her arms. "This isn't our life. Our purpose and understanding transcend way beyond anything we've done tonight."

"Oh yeah, and what about them?"

"Them?"

"The ones who aren't us. The ones who aren't as smart or chosen as us," Alice felt her emotions build in her chest again.

"That's not what I said, Alice."

"Then what are you saying exactly, Lenoir. I'm confused. This movement of light. I thought it was supposed to bring everyone together, to make everything equal. Wasn't that supposed to be it?"

"Of course it is," she rested her head back onto Alice's shoulder.

A strategic move, Alice thought. *Now I can't see her face and gauge her reactions.* "Then what makes *you* better?"

"Oh Alice, I never said I was better. I said I was better informed."

"And why are you better informed?"

"Every truth-- every divine truth needs a person that can inform the others. Like a spokesman."

"So, a leader?"

"If that is your preferred name for it."

"What would your preferred name for it be?"

"I'm a representative of the light. I can teach others what it taught me."

"And why are you the representative?"

"Because I was selected."

"To be at the top?"

"It's not a hierarchy, Alice. This is a frameless world we live in; no matter how many ways people try to create their borders. Most people can't realize they don't exist. Do you know what the two absolutes in the entire world are? Darkness and light."

The cab pulled up to Ramona's house. Once they pulled her out of the cab, she was able to stumble to her front door. Alice saw her inside and made sure she was comfortable for the remainder of the night. When she closed Ramona's door quietly behind her, she looked at Lenoir, waiting in the cab. The moon had risen sometime between their conversation. It was not full, but nearly so. Its beams seemed to bathe the almost desaturated yellow cab in light.

[94]

Lenoir was peering up at it. Alice approached the cab, exhausted from the evening. She decided right then and there, watching her lost friend interact with the otherworldly and otherwise blissful luminosity, that it was a force more powerful than Lenoir behind the psychobabble that she produced. Someone was pulling her strings. She just didn't realize it. Alice was no longer sure she could make her see it without outside help, for she was too far gone.

Since she was just around the corner from Ramona's house, the ride home was silent. Even the driver became dismayed by the radio and chose to roll down his window to let the sounds of the silent streets in. As Alice began to exit, Lenoir wished her a good night.

Reluctantly, Alice said, "You have the same. I hope you are okay going forward, Noir, I really do."

Lenoir beamed along with the moon, "Don't worry about me. I really will be fine, Alice."

"I hope so. It could get very lonely there at the top."

Part 5
Purified Love

So, where are you?

How far does the abyss go down? How thick does the weave of your dedication have to be? It is only through these struggles against darkness and your resistance to the false idols of lure that you can emit light.

The middle point in any journey can be fraught with temptation, frustration and second guesses. None of the indictments flowing through your mind hold true. They will, only if you allow them too. For it is you who guides us to the light, and it is you who it flows seamlessly without shadows or other earthly obstructions.

As we learned in Maakan, love is the only force that can bring along those ready to accept the light. Isik showed only but a glimpse of the light and love that was gifted to you. Allow it to purify and rectify your misgivings. Allow the light in. Always remember, they can see you, they will not let the shadows fulfill what could not be fulfilled in Maakan.

Do not let others confuse your quest and slow you down by tricking you into objections. They know your name and will attempt to call you buy your sins. The light knows your sins but will call you by your true name. When you came to us--nay, when you came to them, you were at a loss of even who you were. Now is the brightest you have ever shined. For you have purpose, objectives, resources, love and above all, light. Not just your own internal flame, which burns like the cold and swells like a wave inside of you. You have the light of all of us behind you.

After your fanfare, the song of a new swan will sing. A larger, more powerful song that will carry throughout the ages, inviting the new to embrace the love and light you have brought them. They will regard you as they regard their own lives and loves, with the upmost honor. They will empathize with those who fell short but praise them for catching an unblemished glimpse.

Always remember where you came from, but also what took you away. Remember what brought you to them. Remember the love and sorrow you feel for those who cannot see.

Remember that the eternal light will inevitably end up where it always belonged. The people.

The dull throb of pain settled again as Vincent awoke in a tangle of sweaty sheets and ice-cold extremities.

He pulled back his only safeguard from his most recent nightly terrors and forced himself up. It had been the last thing on his mind, but the first thing on his priority list—the office. He had to go. There were no two ways about it. Yet still, his heart ached for his family and its future. He hadn't been this shaken since Pamela died. Even then there was a warmer feeling of situational closure. This thing with Lenoir, he had no idea where or how it would end.

Halfway to the bathroom he stopped and said his version of a prayer. He had been dazed. Everyone had seen it. His associates, his daughters, his friends. He had crawled through the holiday season like a blind mouse through a test tube. Overcome, unsure of what came next, immune to the bigger picture and the life that still continued around the fanfare without his knowledge.

He was only able to crack his emotional armor when he noticed the blood mixing with the toothpaste he spat back into the sink. As a doctor had once informed him in his 40s, stress wreaks havoc on the mouth. It causes gums to bleed, capillaries to burst and the roots to disown their rightly place in the mouth.

Alone and shivering from any sort of warmth the world had to offer in January, he sat and looked upon the black terminal screen in his office. Any sort of heartfelt semblance, even that of the electricity at his workstation seemed to be too much. Vincent had been known to punish himself in the past. When Pam died, when Piper first had to go into therapy. But to fail the daughter that hardly had ever needed an inkling of guidance before was too much to bear.

There was just one thing he had to take care of, then he could politely brush aside his secretary who was waiting patiently to deliver him any number of messages. Vincent could no doubt guess what the messages would say too. After all, he had been in this business for a number of years now, and he had grown bored with it. He could perform almost any task it required in his sleep.

He was sure his associates had ceased including him in the regular rotation of leads. They must have been plenty pissed too, because they had stopped calling him. Not that he answered any of the messages they had left, but in his more lucid moments, he had at least been able to listen to them. This was why he had to come in. The firm was in danger of losing one of their biggest accounts. If he could just schedule a meeting and somehow make it there prepared, he could show both his associates and himself that he still wasn't completely worthless.

The account, a local school district, hadn't made it easy to dodge. However many times his associates and friends pinged his phone, the rep for the school district had called at least twice as often. He had been able to make excuses except for yesterday afternoon when he had Piper knowingly lie for him. When she questioned his decision, he thought he better come in and at least make an attempt at amends. He owed it to his company, and he owed it to himself.

He perused the schedule that the rep left with his secretary. Focusing in on the areas when they weren't available. According to the schedule, this morning was one of the embargoed times. He dialed the number while thinking back to a couple weeks ago when Lenoir had a few friends over. Several odd things struck him that night, but he couldn't put a finger on anyone of them. He was trying to remember what he had for dinner that night, wondering if it had been some kind of indigestion before the rep answered.

He sat frozen, trying to conjure up the exact moment of time and his place there before muttering, "Hi Peyton, this is Vincent Adams."

"Ah the ever-illusive Mr. Adams, it's so nice to talk to you!"

"It's nice to finally talk to you too."

"I do wish you could have called."

"Well, I had some time out of the office, you know how the holidays are. To tell you the truth one of my daughters is in the middle of a crisis-" he stopped short of going any further. "But that's all hearsay," he laughed nervously, feeling out of his realm but slowly working back toward his tradesman persona.

"We are still interested if you have the time," Peyton played it cool, putting the ball in his court.

"Absolutely," Vincent nodded while shuffling some papers around, making himself sound busy. In truth he was only staring at his calendar for the next month, it was painstakingly barren. He wondered at that moment if his associates had been at his desk and noticed how bare January looked. He was tempted to fill in false appointments and scheduled meetings in there to make it not look so pathetic – to buy himself a little more time for whatever came next. "I think we could put something on the calendar near the end of the month. That is my soonest availability."

"Hmmm," the ever-patient Peyton hummed. "We were hoping to move on this a bit sooner than that. It won't take very long if you could squeeze in a coffee or even a quick informal weekend meeting to go over the details."

Vincent shuffled more papers, transferring a facsimile he had received in November back and forth across his desk. "I know I'd like to be able to be more accommodating. But I am really crunched. And with this family issue I don't want to put something on the docket only to have to take it right back off again."

She sighed, "How about today? Even if you have 15 minutes between other appointments?"

"Today?" Vincent cringed at how he sounded.

"Yes, I have room this afternoon after lunch. Would that be a possibility? I have all my notes in my car already."

"Today could actually work," he winced. *What are you doing!?* His mind asked. *Today will most certainly not work! Tell her! Make her understand!*

"Excellent, Mr. Adams. I promise I won't take much of your time. Shall we say *The Family Bean*, I know that is out by you? I could be there anytime between one and three."

"You know the more I'm looking at today, maybe that is not such-"

"Oh please, I can just stop by your office too. Ten minutes just to give you the most basic details."

"I just have this feeling that something could come up and I'd hate to leave you-"

"Oh please, Mr. Adams, you couldn't offend me. I will plan on one so you can get to your other appointments. It must be so nice to be so busy. Not the usual after the holidays. But it's a new era, isn't it?"

"A new era?" Vincent repeated.

"Indeed," Peyton giggled. "I will let you get back to it, but I really look forward to going over things at one. See you then!" She didn't wait for Vincent to ramble on with another excuse, she simply disconnected the line.

Vincent, lost in a daze and thinking about this supposed new era had the phone to his ear until the off-hook tone thundered in his ear.

He knew it was wrong and bad business practice to say the least. He knew his associates would be disappointed that he couldn't reel in this account-- which was basically jumping right into their boat-- which in this business was a scarcity. Maybe the all-too-trusting Peyton was right, Vincent thought. Maybe this was indeed a new era.

Despite his dim awareness of what she meant, Vincent could not get away from this other issue.

Unsurprisingly, when the clock struck one, he found himself pouring over microfiche at the Garfield Park Library. He was searching in vain for any kind of reasoning that would set his mind at ease. Something that said it was all misunderstood or a misinterpretation. But a new era? The phrase put him ill at ease. They had been saying the same thing on the news for months now. Ever since those towers all the way across the country had dropped.

Shades of black, white and sometimes monochromatic slides flashed across the screen. He tried to keep his eyes sharp as his fingers adjusted the knob to speed up when it was evident he was nearing a dead end. He was at one corner of the library where the microfiche stations were positioned, surrounded by old men reading newspapers.

Vincent had not heard much about the People's Eternal Light. Just two sentence summarizations in audio clips on the radio or small blurbs in the newspaper. So many of these groups had been talked about, but it was hard to put faces to an organization or even link crimes to specific groups. The librarian had left him with the last six months of The Jerusalem Post. Vincent figured if he couldn't find anything during that period, there would be no point in looking any further. After all, the world's interest in these kinds of matters had only just begun.

Countless stories about Aleph, the Raëlian church, the Order of the Solar Temple whizzed by, as well as retro pieces on Heaven's Gate, Unification Church and Branch Davidians. Another dozen or so nationalist groups and something else called SOTES, but nothing on the People's Eternal Light.

With his eyes bleary and his face starting to sweat, Vincent stood from the hot seat. Instead of handing back the spools of microfiche to the librarian, he took a lap to clear his head. When that didn't work, he slurped water out of a nearby drinking fountain. Even though his general sense told him not to, he also checked his phone that informed him that he had had eight missed calls in the last hour. *Sorry Peyton,* he muttered under his breath as he sat back down to get to work.

Minutes gave way to another hour and by the time he thought he would never make it through his research, he came upon the last spool. It was labeled *J Post August 2001-Present. Here goes nothing,* he thought.

He breezed past sections that wouldn't hold what he sought out, sections like regional, entertainment, sports, business. He was really only looking at the news and editorial sections. There was one interesting piece in world news that listed that reporter's recent research of sects in the area of Damascus. There was one on his list called "The benefaction of eternal light," but little other information. After taking a pause and searching online at a computer terminal and coming up with nothing, Vincent returned to his seat again.

He was about to give up, cursing himself for missing the meeting with Peyton and instead wasting his entire afternoon and getting no closer to the truth when he saw it. The headline read in big block letters, Local tribunals in the Dark on People's light. This article was written from Jerusalem by a reporter from the associated press. It discussed a nearby region on the outskirts of the city called Anata.

> *The marketplace was bustling with every kind of person you'd want to meet in Jerusalem. All languages here are spoken, all dialects accepted. Places of worship are also commonplace to the people of Anata. Places of worship that are stationary and also mobile. Today the latter variety take their places before dawn to obtain the best corner to spread their word. The usual subsects of Christianity are here, as well as several Islamic groups. But there are also the white robed ministers and their followers that*

the locales have only heard about through word of mouth. These people of the eternal light, as they call themselves, have concentrated near the holy city for many months now. They were known to state officials who track such groups in previous years as a soft target, as they had no history of violence or malice in the past.

This classification has changed according to such officials over the past few years. In this age of terrorism, now they are taking a closer look at the People of the Eternal Light. "They come to this market every morning, they line up and prey on people that are easily influenced," one official who wanted to remain anonymous stated to me. "They bring back a dozen or so with them at dusk, we never see them again because they send them to another camp."

According to the locales, the People of the Eternal Light have been seen out in the unforgiving desert, erecting temples and holding gatherings that last all night and day. Loud music and wanderlust seem to accompany them wherever they go. Propaganda on how to live one's life according to the light has been strewn throughout these marketplace-- pamphlets that passerbyers receive when they cross paths with these travelers of the light.

"They have traveled everywhere, and it shows in their members," the official confided in me later. "I even saw several Westerners among them." Apparently, talks have been taking place among regional nations on these types of groups that they call כת ;פולחן or cults to Western readers. According to the ICSA (International Cultic Studies Association), a worldwide organization that tracks organizational activities such as the People's Light, a cult earns its title if it has at least three of the following criteria:

Members are encouraged to display unquestioning commitment to its leadership.

Questioning of group practices can cause a member to be ostracized, punished or banished.

The leadership dictates how members should think, act, feel and many other choices concerning their daily lives.

The group is elitist, often claiming a special status for themselves.

The group exhibits a polarized us versus them mentality in their actions and rhetoric.

The leadership is not accountable to any authority.

The group teaches members that its end purpose justifies all of their means, leading members to behave and act in ways deemed reprehensible prior to membership with the group.

The leadership encourages feelings of shame, guilt and/or joy and praise in order to influence and/or control members.

The group is preoccupied with bringing in new members.

Members are encouraged or required to live and/or socialize only with other group members.

I showed the list to the local official here in Jerusalem. When I asked him if the People's Light showed any of these characteristics, he only nodded, all of them, *he indicated. Despite the group being entrenched in Anata, officials are still trying to gather information on them. While the official did not want to go on record, he did indicate that authorities from the local tribunals are looking into missing person cases related to the group. "When interviewing witnesses related to these cases, it is hard to pinpoint information," he explained. "It can be similar to interviewing witnesses to organized crime or domestic violence. The victims, nor their people do*

[106]

not want to share information that could help these investigations for fear of retribution."

I asked the local official what could be useful to them in investigating these groups further. "Collaborations from other jurisdictions and organizations." The tribunals are themselves sharing information, but it can be hard for these agencies to obtain information from other countries. With the People's Light constantly on the move, with different memberships of the group popping up around the Middle East and even as far away as Eastern Europe and the Mediterranean, officials in Jerusalem hope that the politics and infighting can be put aside. No one wants to admit that these groups can infiltrate their communities, thus no one will admit there are ongoing issues in their communities. "This needs to change," the official stated gravely. "These groups destroy families; they use people and then throw them away. They perpetuate violence, both directly and indirectly. They also use drug substances in their rituals, as well as other amoral practices. If those who have had direct contact cannot help us stop them, then who can we turn to?"

Last week, a body of a young Chinese woman was discarded in an alley not from the marketplace. She was found a long way from home in a white robe. Of course, no one from the area of Anata knows the woman, and officials are still working to identify-

"Vincent, is that you?" A woman's voice called out to him. He hadn't noticed that his knees were bumping the table involuntarily and his cushioned library chair was now soaked with sweat. He looked up to see Meredith Nielsen looking back at him. Her eyes wide with anticipation and dressed to the nines in a form fitting t shirt, leggings and the latest footwear fad, crocs.

[107]

"Meredith, hi!" Vincent feigned excitement in his voice even though he was in a special kind of hell. He jumped out of his chair to give her a hug and instantly regretted it when mid-embrace felt his shirt slick with sweat stick to her skin. "I hope Bill is treating you well."

"He's doing a good job for us, all the partners are really happy!" she beamed. Meredith was always full of joy as if she had an infinite supply. "Bill is great, but he's not as good as you Vincent."

"Well," he smiled, "I had so much on my plate, I had to send Bill some referrals or he'd never forgive me."

"What a great problem to have this day in age," she touched his shoulder lightly. She did not seem the slightest bit perturbed by his bewildered and frantic state. Or perhaps, doubtfully, but perhaps he was covering it better than he thought.

Vincent found his eyes tracking back to the microfiche screen when he saw his spool of articles moving forward at a leisurely pace. He must have hit the knob, which had a hare trigger, when he jumped up to greet Meredith. "Oh no," he muttered, halting the rotating articles.

"Oh," Meredith purred, "Did you lose your spot? What are you working on right now?"

"Oh nothing," Vincent waved it off. "Just something for a client."

"Oh, those lucky ducks! Getting your expertise is a high commodity these days it seems. You know even though you do not have room on your schedule, I would love to have dinner sometime and catch up."

"Well Meredith that is a very kind offer, but when we tried that last time, I think we found-"

"You know what? I have to dart off, but please let me know how you are doing. Give me a call Vincent. Sometimes what you are looking for is in the place you least expect it," she laid down her business card in front of the microfiche machine, "my cell number is on the back," she gave him another quick hug and took flight, out of the library like a bat out of hell. The more Vincent thought about it given what he saw on display on their first date two years ago, he was sure her joy came in the form of the Adderall she was prescribed on top of the many cappuccinos she consumed throughout her business ventures.

He sat back down in a huff, inadvertently spinning the knob on the microfiche machine so that the articles doubled back from their previous position. He wished he had hit print on the article. Now it would take him another half hour to find it. Once he did, he took it as a sign for the rest of his day. He packed up the microfiche, returned it to the librarian and made his own mad dash away from the Garfield Park Library.

Later, at home his head was still spinning. He had reread the article several times over at stoplights and in traffic. Even this field reporter from the article only gave vague hints of this organization, what they believed in and what they have done to make sure others believed it too. It was so full of hypocrisy, but so unfocused it seemed at the same time. Whoever was in charge seemed to be good at keeping their extracurricular activities secret.

BUT, a voice screamed at Vincent from his mind's eye, *THEY HAVE YOUR DAUGHTER SO YOU NEED TO FIND OUT.*

Vincent didn't realize he was pacing, but he let out a growl of frustration when he realized the brevity of what this voice told. It was an absolutely maddening situation! They had his daughter, but they didn't at the same time. She was right here, and had been for a couple of months now, under his very roof where he could watch her. But the only thing he had been watching her do is slip further away. He had spent so many years worrying about Lenoir (as she was his first child and daughter), but while she was gone, and this was what may have been stinging Vincent the most, he hardly paid her a thought at all. He was busy building his career, which he was now sabotaging because Lenoir was back? It made no sense, and it was hardly her fault. He felt guilty having these feelings, and with no outlet to turn to, he grabbed a stack of saltines out of the cupboard and began inhaling them at an alarming rate whilst thinking about how to save his daughter.

How could he find out what world journalists and ambassadors and other men of international relations could not? And why couldn't they find out? Was it that this group was still operating under the radar, that none of the crimes talked about in the article could be tied to them or that they simply just didn't care?

If they couldn't find out, then it was quite simple, Vincent would. But how?

YOU ARE GOING TO HAVE TO DIG A LITTLE DEEPER THAN THE PUBLIC LIBRARY. That voice was right there again, full of answers.

"Start with what you know," he told himself aloud. "Start with those who know her best," he added.

The doorbell rang out then, a church bell sound that seemed to reverberate throughout the empty, hollow house. He wondered as he wiped the saltine crumbs off his shirt if anyone else was home. Maybe Lenoir herself was there. If she was seriously under the control of conspiring minds, would she be able to hear his thoughts? Predict his actions?

He paused long enough to listen in case any movement occurred upstairs, but when none presented itself, the doorbell rang again. He stepped into the foyer and tore the door open, as if he had been ding-dong ditched hundreds of times by relentless neighborhood kids with a penchant for mischief.

As he looked upon Lenoir's good friend Alice, standing alone in the doorway, looking like a deer in headlights or a lost child shivering in a forlorn gutter

[110]

somewhere, Meredith's hyper-caffeinated fueled words came back to him from earlier in the afternoon. "Alice?" he sounded extremely surprised.

"I hope this isn't a bad time," she said meekly.

"Well if you're looking for Lenoir, she isn't here."

"She isn't. I- I think I need to talk to you about her."

"Oh?" Vincent noticed an errant cracker crumb he had missed and quickly discarded it without her noticing. "Come on in. Can I offer you anything?"

"Sure," Alice nodded while blindly stumbling through the doorway. She looked like she had tunnel vision, she could only see what was right in front of her, and it wasn't Vincent.

She sat down in the very den he had seen her the last time. That day had been so much different than the present one. It was late November, and everyone was filled with such joy and the sight of the lost Lenoir returning home. Alice stared off in the distance, looking past the walls of his temporary holding cell of a home, which was what it felt like now. She looked positively disturbed.

"So, what's going on in Lenoir's life?" he tried to keep it breezy and jovial.

"I wish I knew," the grave look of concern still on her face.

"I'm sure it's not as bad as all that."

"She does seem very different than before she left."

"Of course," he nodded, "You girls are at an age where tons of things are changing in your life." He cringed slightly inward, thinking he sounded like such an old man.

"To be perfectly honest," Alice drew a breath, "I think there is something wrong. I think she has been manipulated in some way. The things she talks about, the words she uses. They don't sound like her own," Alice was upset. It seemed she may be on the verge of tears.

Vincent sat, dumbfounded, repeating the contents of the article over and over again in his head. Thinking about

Meredith. What had she said? *Sometimes what you are looking for is in the place you least expect it.* Something along those lines? But surely it doesn't have anything to do with Lenoir, or even Alice. Meredith was most likely talking about herself. She was dropping a hint that she wanted to continue seeing him. And like the dope he has been acting like all day, he completely missed it.

"You've seen it too. You must have. Don't you think the old Lenoir would be going a million miles an hour onto her next phase. That was how she was. Remember her in high school? First, she wanted to be in band, and she got first chair for cello. But then she lost interest right away, so she moved onto gymnastics until that got too boring for her. Then it was onto debate."

"Which she has always certainly excelled at, believe me," Vincent chuckled while his insides were afire.

"My point is, the old Lenoir would be applying for college, or getting a job, or off joining the peace corps. Don't you think it is funny how comfortable she has been just standing pat? It seems to me that she does have a plan, like she always would. If so, what is she waiting for? And why isn't she talking about it at all?" She sipped the water Vincent had brought out for her. She seemed to be shaking all over, but something about her also seemed calmer than when he first glimpsed out on the front porch.

"Well Alice-" he began, although he had no idea where he was going with it. His mind was racing with a thousand thoughts per second, and damned if he knew how to slow them down. "I guess I haven't seen much of what you said. Initially, I had a feeling like something was wrong, but- I talked to Peyton's therapist about it a little. He put my mind at ease. He told me how big of an adjustment that living abroad is for years and then coming back. It's not like flipping a light switch. It will take some fine-tuning. I think we can let Lenoir have a little space. I think she's earned that." The words came out of someone else's mouth, not his. As he was reciting the words, he looked at Alice and realized she was way too smart to fall for this. And why was he resisting her help? She was no longer a child. Wasn't she the very thing he has needed all day long? Now that she was here, he was sabotaging it again, just like the career he had built. At that point, Vincent wasn't sure if his mind had collapsed based on his worry for his daughter or worry for himself. Because it was quite clear he too was starting to go off the rails.

She stared at him, not showing any emotion. It was kind of frightening to see a look from Alice who was young and should not yet have gone through the turmoil of the years it takes to perfect that look. He also remembered she was no dolt. In fact, she was likely the smartest of Lenoir's friends. All of that plus the day he had, he was pretty sure she saw right through his speech.

"Are you sure I can't offer you some tea or coffee," he asked her. "Kind of wet out there, isn't it?"

"I-" Alice stammered. "I don't know what I'm looking for," she placed her hands over her own face.

"Sometimes what you are looking for is in the place you least expect it," he repeated Meredith's mantra blandly, like a set of song lyrics that were stuck in his head.

She looked up at him for the first time with a faint glint of hope in her eyes.

He too sat up straighter as if it was the first time he understood the meaning behind those words. *What is happening to you?* His mind's eye barked again. He ignored it. This revelation or whatever it was was more powerful. "What exactly is it that Lenoir said or did not say?"

"It's hard to tell," she shook her head. "Every time I ask her about it, she has a way of circling the conversation back. When I press her, she has this special way of not answering but pretending that she did."

Vincent chuckled, "Tell me about it. She's always been like that. She has inherited her mother's stubborn persona." It hit him hard just then. He realized something else at that moment. There was no way he could lose her like he had lost his wife. That was this sudden rush of heroism he felt. It is why he spent all day looking for a needle in a haystack and dodging calls from Peyton. It was why he was having this discussion with Alice now.

"The weirdest thing are these people she meets with," Alice said matter-of-factly. "They come and go, and she never introduces us, she hardly even acknowledges they exist. I think she thinks she is better at keeping secrets than she is."

"What people?" Vincent scooted forward in his seat.

"These people wearing these white robes. Some have beards and are older. Some are women. Most are foreign, but some look American."

"How many of them have you seen?"

"At least 5, but maybe 6 or 7." Then Alice broke loose. The tears began to flow, but she continued talking, ignoring her own pain. "I've tried to get Scarlett and Ramona to see, but they can't. I've tried so hard to talk to Lenoir, but she is unreachable. She has been acting like she is being completely open, but she is so closed off. I don't know what else to do, but I think there is danger coming for her."

"What do you mean danger?"

"Why else would she not acknowledge the people in white robes?"

Vincent let out a sigh. It was all so cryptic, yet so familiar. The article in *Jerusalem Post* had mentioned people in white robes. This unfortunate information session with Alice should have sent him off the deep end, but he felt a bit of relief knowing he was not the only one who saw it now. It made him feel less crazy. He could also sense that Alice was in desperate need of this relief as well. "Okay, I'm going to show you what I found at the library today. Tell me if it means anything to you."

He showed her the article. She read it carefully, slowly, absorbing the information it detailed. She was taking a while, so he figured she re-read it. Thoughts of Lenoir drifted through his mind. Things *were* beginning to add up. The variables consisted of every strange smile she fed him when he asked if there was anything he could do or help her with. It showed up when he would mention a story about her mother or something that happened when she was young – it was always met with this strained showing of emotion that was not at all genuine. Vincent hated thinking ill of his own daughter. He constantly had to remind himself that it wasn't her fault. Even the article alluded to it. Foreigners in a foreign land. People like Lenoir who are fully ready to commit to a cause if they find some small part of it to believe in – and that's all it takes. If her mind was being held captive – no – of course he would never blame her. He was doing what he should have a long time ago before she even went on this adventure of hers.

When Alice was finished, another wistful tear dropped down before she wiped it away. "You know, I think I will take that tea if you are still offering."

He brought it back to her and she sipped it gingerly as it all came out. She told him a story about her father and what had happened to his family when he was young. How his brother, Alice's Uncle, was one of the smartest men they had known, and he too was taken in by way of some kind of emotional and spiritual control. "It just goes to show you that anyone can be victimized. Vulnerability of the mind has nothing to do with intelligence."

This story scared Vincent even more, but he thanked her for telling him. They talked more, not necessarily about Lenoir, but more philosophical about what it means to have control of your own life. It was not a conversation he would have thought he would have with anyone, let alone little

Alice Crutchfield who he knew as only a shy girl who would always call him Mr. Adams no matter how much he told her not to. As they talked, she kept asking him what they should do, but he had no answer. He was still trying to wrap his head around the information he had learned throughout the day.

At the front door, he gave her an umbrella because the rain had picked up. She asked once again, "So what are we going to do?"

He shook his head, "Nothing. I think I have learned all that I need to learn about the 'People's Eternal Light' for one day. I just wanted to thank you Alice for coming here tonight. I'm sorry I put up such a shield. I was honestly just lost, and that is something I don't like to admit very often."

"Me either," she nodded. "It doesn't make me feel like a very capable friend or person."

"Or father," he agreed. "I think we should just wait and see. I will try to have more of a frank discussion with my daughter. Maybe coming from me, it could be different. Maybe not, I don't know."

"I just feel better knowing that I'm not the only one anymore."

"You certainly are not. We will get more help if we need it. I'll hire a damn deprogrammer if I have to. We'll take her if she won't come willingly. I will not let her go."

"Thank you, Mr. Adams."

"I know it won't do any good, but please call me Vincent."

She laughed and thanked him again before exiting.

After Alice had left, Vincent poured himself a couple of fingers of whiskey. It was something he usually only drank in the company of friends or colleagues, but he felt he wanted it tonight in order to wind his mind down. After he finished, he ventured upstairs and checked to make sure no one else was home. Piper was in her room listening to music and chatting with friends online, but she was not interested in anything but AOL and Eminem – so he let her be.

Later, he parked himself in front of the TV and fell asleep. The witching hour had approached, and the wind and rain were fiercely howling outside. He heard her come in through the front. He was dazed, but still found it odd that she looked stressed and was bone dry despite the weather.

"Where were you?" he asked sheepishly. He had a strange sensation in his head that he could tell was beginning to turn into a headache, likely from the whiskey.

"I've been out all day. Did you fall asleep?" she dropped her purse and joined him on the couch.

He pulled himself up from his slump with a grunt. He straightened up, getting his bearings, figuring out how he could look at her without drawing ire, or suspicion. Then it all came back to him in a flood of ill-advised memories. The newspaper article had gotten him worried, the conversation with Meredith had caught him off guard, but the visit with Alice and all she had shared with him had put him over the edge. "I guess I must have," he muttered.

"Everything okay?" she asked cheerily.

He glanced at the TV and then tried to rub the sleep out of his eyes. He had left the television on CNN. John Walker Holmes' picture was up in the background while a well-groomed talking head in a clip-on suit chattered erratically giving his two cents about the whole ordeal. Then footage of him being led off a US military plane cut in. He looked strained and beaten down, his head hung low. He tried to shield his face from the cameras surrounding him. Vincent could sympathize with that feeling. It was the same way he felt at that moment when he looked at his daughter and knew what he had to ask her. He slowly shook his head, feeling the burn in his eyes, which were dry and scratchy.

"Dad," she crossed her arms while he stared on like a fish looking out of its glass tank. "What's wrong?"

He studied her to see if there was real feeling behind her question, scrutinizing her reactions and features. "I don't know quite how to bring it up," he said slowly.

Just then, Piper entered from the kitchen carrying a tray of leftover slices of sausage and crackers. She sat down next to her sister, who squeezed next to Vincent, forcing him to make room.

"Hey sister dear," Lenoir smiled at her while stealing two crackers and a slice of sausage to make a sandwich.

"Hey!" Piper grabbed at her hands, but it was too late.

"You know, when I was in Shileh the locals had a saying, "*Happiness isn't perfect until it's shared.*"

"Well, this isn't happiness its food," Piper stuck her tongue out at her.

"Why may I ask do you eat it then?" Lenoir challenged.

"It tastes good, and I'm hungry."

"What would you say it brings you?"

"A full stomach," Piper creased her forehead, not understanding.

"Fulfillment. Good. Did you know that the Maharishi said, '*Life finds its fulfillment in the expansion of happiness.*'?"

"He also hung out with the Beatles a lot," Piper quipped, "What's your point?"

They both laughed then. Perhaps it was the absurdity of their conversation or just how stubborn and unrelenting they both were being. Either way, Vincent did not laugh, his headache expanded itself. He felt like the walls of his skull were closing in on his brain, squeezing it until it would pop, not giving him enough time to-

[118]

"What's wrong with Dad? The yard guy miss another hedge?"

"I don't know, he won't tell me," Lenoir shrugged.

"Piper, would you please excuse us for a moment?" Vincent said without any humor in his voice, souring the mood.

"Why?" Piper protested, shoving in the last cracker from the tray.

"Because I asked you to. I need to talk to your sister."

"So, talk to her, why do I gotta go?"

"Yeah dad," Lenoir grabbed Piper by the shoulders. "Anything you say to me I'm just going to tell her anyway; you know how sisters are."

"Piper, please go up to your room now. I'll explain later."

"God!" Piper stomped out, "I thought I was supposed to be the moody one." She threw her tray into the kitchen sink with a clung and her footfalls made sure they were heard the rest of the way through the hall, up the stairs and into her room."

Vincent stared at Lenoir, thinking she looked more grown up now then she ever did before. She showed concern, but still kept on smiling with that grin she wore ever since she had come back.

"Dad, you've been acting weird lately, but it's no reason to take it out on Piper. After all, this one dude I met in Jodhpur, he was Belgian, he said that when you feel-"

"Lenoir, I really am not in the mood to hear another word of wisdom or hear about the latest mediation technique right now."

Her true expression stayed blank, but she arched her eyebrows in an overly animated manner. "Okay. But I thought you wanted to talk to me?"

"I do. I do. I'm sorry. I know I haven't been acting like myself lately," he rubbed his temples. "To tell you the truth I haven't felt like myself."

"You should get more exercise. The best way to lift your spirit is to-" she stopped herself. "Sorry," she added.

He blinked at her and shook his head again. "I'm just at a loss. It's not too often your old dad doesn't have the slightest idea what to do, but look upon it, because here it is."

"I'm sure it's not as bad as that," she hugged him. "You been to the doctor lately?" she asked calmly.

"No, but that's not it."

"Then what?" her voice never strained; it was as if she were just going through the motions.

He stared at the TV another minute. The news had moved onto showing footage of Lindh in his first US court hearing. It was intercut with several pictures of him in Afghanistan fighting and training with the Taliban, back when he still had his long beard and Islamic garb. "What do you think about this clown?" he asked her. "Grew up in a nice house up in Washington, came from a regular family - a family just like us. He played sports in school, listened to rap music, went online to talk to his friends, just like Piper does now. And then they find him like this," he outstretched his hand when the news feed cut to a picture of him hiding in a hole where the US military found him.

Lenoir stayed silent next to him, but she looked at the screen. Vincent turned to look at her intently, but then she glanced back to him.

"He was just a regular kid," he whispered to her. "How could it have gotten to that point?"

"I've met a lot of Islamic people in my travels. It's a very powerful force that like many forces do some good, and some bad."

"Yeah, but what about what he did? To the country I mean."

"It looks as if he will have his day in court," Lenoir gestured to the television. "But his true judgment comes when his light extinguishes."

"What judgment?"

"I thought you didn't want to hear about all that, dad."

"Right," Vincent said, picking up the remote and starting to flip through channels. He did it slow at first, as if he didn't have a destination in mind, but once he realized how far off the news channels were, he flipped faster and faster. He stopped when he reached footage of 9/11 on MSNBC. The planes torpedoing into the towers were burned in everyone's mind, only because they played the footage over and over again as if it were an instant replay at the Superbowl. "What about 9/11 then?"

"Jeez padre, you're full of rosy topics today. What about it?"

"What did you first think about when you heard the news?"

"I felt badly for the people involved."

"The victims," Vincent nodded. "A lot of people died that day."

"The victims, the police, the perpetrators themselves. Such misguided servitude."

"What?"

"The men. The Saudis. They were willing to give their lives up and they didn't even know what for. There was no honor in what they did," Lenoir shook her head. "They didn't even know why they did it. They only did it because they were told to."

"You think there ever would be a good reason to do something like that?"

"I think that there is honor in standing up and calling attention to a belief. But that's just it. The men who gave the order to them were calling attention to darkness, to depravity."

"What do you mean?" he asked, growing frustrated.

"Their darkness lied in their intentions, and their intentions masqueraded as a calling. Both were false. False prophets are about as far away as you can get from the light. If you're going to commit to an act of proclamation, especially an aggressive one, you better be sure you are filled with enough light to see why you're doing it. Otherwise, what is the point?" She looked to him for support.

He tried to figure out what on earth she was talking about, but he had just woken up. It was not going well. This heart to heart he was having with his daughter. He pictured it in the morning over coffee, not in front of the dim shadows of the idiot box with a hangover brewing. It was going as well as it had gone for Alice, the way she described it. His daughter had built a wall with no trusted access, only twists and turns and never-ending paths that led to nowhere.

"Lenoir," he said slowly so that he would not be misunderstood. "I don't think I need to tell you that murder and inflicting terror upon an entire nation is never acceptable."

"You think it doesn't go on everywhere? It happens in every corner of the world. That is why we can expose it for what it is. I'm sure some kind of terror was inflicted upon the men who carried this out, or their families. What would you do in their situation? How would you expose this awful pattern? Words only work when they fall upon ears willing to listen. How often have you found that happening to you dad?"

He sat, stunned at the words coming out of his daughter's mouth. His daughter who when she was six gave her entire allowance to a kid at school who said he didn't have a lunch. Lenoir who once gave him and Piper and the woman he was dating at the time, certificates of donations to the local food shelf for Christmas instead of presents. But then, he remembered the time she used her fists on a bully picking on her classmate in the 5th grade. There was also the time she thought her friend Stella had been unfairly suspended from school, so she had taken pictures of her principal's car, private home and children and sent them to him through the mail in a threatening manner. He had forgotten about that incident. Lenoir was going through a particularly moody phase early in high school. The police had to get involved, but Lenoir swore up and down that it was just a childish prank coerced by her friends.

Vincent could think of a hundred different arguments for each side to her and countless stories to support both. Was this darkness in his daughter from the beginning, only he just wasn't objective enough to see it? Or has this influence been transplanted from some third world gutter philosophy spewing reptile that has sunk its claws into her while she was overseas and off his radar? How could he be certain? What would he have to do to find out?

"It's not going to work you know," she said to him finally after a long lapse of silence and his mental retreat.

"What isn't?"

"You can't have her back," she whispered to him and quietly left him in the den to be with his thoughts. "She belongs to Isik now. She belongs to the light."

Part 6
Too Close For Comfort

So, where are you?

How is it that we find you here again? How many times will the Temple in Maakan continue to call you back to the light? They have been tolerant, overly empathetic in their pursuit to bring your plans to achievement.

You don't blame them for requiring progress. For wanting answers. Their relief in sending the others with you will not, however, atone for your own resolute obstruction of your work.

The light's work.

Brought to interest by your own ambitions and dreams. Has this unsophisticated world of simplistic perversions and crooked profiteering spirited you away again? Are you really so susceptible in thinking those who question your logic will be there for you when the world goes dark?

What is it you are expecting from them? Their misgivings crack the foundation that holds everything you have accomplished. Are you going to let them walk the fool's stride? Trotting over your control of this life? This mission?

We don't know how else to call you. Other than the refrain that Maakan loves you.

Isik loves you.

His love is like an expanding light careening across the skies, waiting for you to signal that you are ready to accept.

They are waiting for you. For your signal.

To send it, you only need to let go of your own misgivings.

The fear of the light will be too immense if you cannot push forward. So many of them *choose* to be lost in the dark. Their conscience may be empty, but their shallow residuals foster a rhetoric that makes the world as bleak as it is. If left to their own devices, they will lead humanity down a burrow of misery.

Did Isik not remind you time and time again that you have the power to make it perfect?

Why don't you trust him? Why are you more inclined to defend a darkness that masquerades itself as a society of fellowship? A society so fearful of the light that they are willing to take you and others like you, parade them in front of the assembly as monsters in order to squash any enthusiasm the future may have.

They ask you about the man in trouble. The one who comes from the same deprivation as you. His failure will highlight your success. Isik compels you to lean on his teachings and recite them with your guardians. After all, it was his words that made up your cries even before he spoke them to you. *Let all men share in the responsibility that caused our current realm to not only exist, but to decay, and allow all women the space and support to heal it. *

From Section 145, unit 17 of the Teachings of Isik

The familiar ringing by this point was like a knife twisting into Vincent's brain. He had been seeing flashes of white strength pushing into his vision the past few days, no doubt from lack of sleep. The only time he was able to sleep was when he took his Ambien. But he hated the stuff, for it causes him great anxiety. That was likely why his mind kept travelling to awful places and he wasn't able to hear what was right in front of him.

"Helllooo?" the voice on the other end of the phone huffed impatiently. "I don't think anyone is there-" the receptionist told a co-worker.

"No wait!" Vincent snapped out of whatever held his attention. "I need to speak to Dr. Cassok, it's urgent."

Silence greeted him on the other end. He was about to repeat his request when she finally said, "Vincent, like I told you two hours ago, two days ago and two weeks ago, Dr. Cassok is on leave, and I don't know yet when he will return."

"But it is an emergency," he muttered, tired of this script.
"If YOU need attention immediately, I can setup an appointment with Dr. Rosenthal."

"But I DON'T KNOW DR. ROSENTHAL!" he tried to keep composed, but it was always one step forward, two steps back. "AND HE DOESN'T KNOW ME OR MY FAMILY. Putting me in touch with someone new will not help. Please! If I could just talk to Dr. Cassok on the phone for two minutes. I know he could help."

"I'm afraid that's impossible."

"There must be something you can do."

"There is nothing I can do, Mr. Adams. If you need emergency assistance, you can go to the emergency room. If it can wait, I can put you in touch with Dr. Cassok's colleague."

"Please," his prickly voice sounded pathetic.

"There is no sense in asking the same questions over and over again, the answers remain the same. And now I have someone here and have to go. Goodbye Mr. Adams." He then heard her add as she replaced the cradle on the receiver, "*until next time.*"

"Please, I don't know what else to do," he confessed to the dial tone.

Vincent Adams was his name and avoidance was his latest game. Whom hadn't he been avoiding lately? As March crept in like a lamb, he realized even his own two daughters had been added to that ever-growing list. He had no idea where he stood at work at this point. He had received fewer calls from the office than he expected. The last time he was there, to errantly grab a coffee mug which still sat on the floor of his car, people seemed to understand and let him be. He wasn't sure what it was they understood - that he was going through a crisis? That his life was unspooling before everyone's eyes? That that very fabric of his family was being torn asunder?

What did he have to show for his leave of absence? Not just from work, but his family? It had been nearly two months since his and Lenoir's last real heart to heart. Ever since, he had been avoiding her with greater prowess. Not that it was difficult to do; she had been more out than in. He received his information through Piper who could barely even look at him anymore.

Lenoir was busy applying for college, taking small trips and "making amends." When he pursued that further, Piper scoffed and flippantly replied, "Why don't you ask her yourself, DAD." She had made sure to emphasize his patriarchal role to rub salt in the wound.

He had also taken a leave of absence from his senses. It turned out Peyton from the school district; his last in a long string of disappointed clients was not so easily dissuaded. She continued ringing Vincent after he stood her up. He had even received a call from his associate Robert Mueller who was civil and empathetic to his situation, but also extremely perplexed at how Vincent could lose such a slam-dunk client so easily. That call came in over six weeks ago, and ever since, his communication with his firm and staff had gone dark.

Finally, it seemed he had taken a leave of absence from himself. His five-o-clock shadow seemed to grow in every time he put the razor to his neck. His hygiene had been less than congenial, or so he thought. If he hadn't been dodging his daughters, he was sure they'd let him know. But why did he torture himself this way? What was the point?

He only needed to look at the kitchen table and what was strewn atop of it to answer that question. Ever since his failure at reaching the one girl he thought he would always connect with, his oldest daughter and forever age accelerator. He looked at the piles of information nestled in their file folders-- information scraped up from the unlikeliest of sources – information that always led him nowhere. He had visited the Garfield Park Library and even the main branch downtown on Church Street countless times. With each visit, he had left with a new stack of literature ranging from psychology textbooks to mind control techniques. He had maybe a dollop more of information on the *People's Eternal Light* than before everything had started. In this information age, it was mind blowing how little was out there on the group.

He even broke out of his technophobe comfort zone and started something called a "message board" for possible contact with other U.S. victims of this enterprise. He took a step toward his latest workstation, shuddering at the amount of information he had poured through. The only thing he had learned since he made this his life's work was the leader's name, Isik. According to an anonymous source, supposedly a member that had escaped with their life and mind intact, his name is Isik Veren, a former citizen of Turkey, although the government's official stance is that they have never heard of him. He has been off the grid for at least ten years according to this source, so no one can corroborate his story. The entirety of the two-sentence statement had been all Vincent had to show for his last eight weeks of insanity.

At his wit's end, he decided he would start working on Lenoir again. She was after all, his best possible chance at information. All he wanted was to undo the damage that had been done. Of course, after delving ever deeper into the psychology of cults, it became apparent that the process was extremely complicated and ineffective.

He would need help.

This revelation made him reach out to Dr. Cassok a few weeks ago, but that only proved to be the latest in an endless string of failed tasks. If he hadn't already been so deranged with hopelessness, he would really start to take it personally.

At mid-morning he had been reviewing a paper by a college student at the American University of Beirut. The paper consisted of antidotes from locals that included information on local cult activity in the Baabda region. This article was presented with a framework that put forth the idea that the locals suffered from mental illness due to particles in the water supply. Vincent did not really care much about the cause, just the stories the locals told, and they told many about strange gatherings at night, wild orgies that brought to mind Sodom and Gomorrah, and high priests influencing young people with this rhetoric. There was no mention of the People's Eternal Light yet, but he had barely made it past the literature review when a knock at the side door derailed him.

The door was hardly used, especially by guests. As Vincent shuffled his printouts into the nearest folder, no longer conscious of organization and the system he had created, he wondered how a guest could even get into the backyard without knowing the security code. He straightened his posture in case it was Lenoir. He supposed now was as good a time as any to hash it out once and for all.

However, after he unbolted the long-locked door and opened it with a creek, there stood an impeccably bereft looking man in a cheap black suit and inquisitive looking eyes. He looked like someone's grandfather who may have been a private investigator and had since retired, but still insisted on wearing the uniform. Unexpectant of this company, Vincent tried to unruffle his morning rooster's comb and straighten his robe, all the while wondering how and why the man gained access to and chose this door.

The man studied him for a beat before opening his mouth, "Mr. Adams, I presume?"

"Yes?" Vincent replied facetiously.

"My name is Oz Nolan, I'm with the agency."

Vincent's heart thundered to a stop, but he showed more composure than he believed he had these days. "Which one?"

The man brought out a black bi-fold wallet from the inside pocket of his coat, displaying what was inside to Vincent, a shiny gold star.

"Oh."

"I wonder if I might have a few minutes of your time," Oz stated, not unkindly.

"Sure," Vincent sounded slightly annoyed, which was likely better for him. He wasn't entirely sure what the man wanted, but his mind prodded him that it would be better to appear annoyed at this intrusion.

"May I come in?" Oz's eye wandered passed Vincent, who was sure he noticed the large stack of file folders on the table.

What would he say or do if he noticed the contents of those folders? After all, this wasn't the time and place in history to be studying the kind of topics he was, especially with a man from *that* agency. "You know," Vincent stepped out and shut the door behind him, "The house is a mess, and I wasn't exactly expecting company. Let's talk out here."

"If it suits you better."

"What does this concern?" Vincent led him to a couple of lawn chairs in the middle of the yard as if it were the most natural place to hold a conversation.

Oz didn't sit and neither did Vincent, they stood holding eye contact until the agency man broke away. "It's a matter of great importance. It's something we could use your help with Mr. Adams. Not to create unnecessary grandeur, but it may even be a matter of national security."

Vincent's heart stopped a second time, he looked around, wondering if the jackboots were already on his property and waiting for Mr. Nolan's word to strike. "That sounds intriguing, but I'm afraid I will need more information than that, if I am to be of any help."

"There's no reason to be nervous, Mr. Adams. There are just a few things we need to clarify and I'm hoping you might be the man to do it."

"I'm all ears."

Oz then decided to sit in the lawn chair after all. Vincent studied him momentarily before accepting the peace offering and sitting beside him. "It's not the easiest of subjects to broach, but I'm afraid I must be forthcoming with you Mr. Adams."
Suddenly he was reminded of Alice, "Please, call me Vincent."

Oz smiled, "Thanks for that Vincent. You know, I raised daughters myself. I know how difficult it can be. I also know the feeling of doing anything to protect them, even if it goes against your better judgment." He waited patiently for a reply, or at the very least a reaction from Vincent.

Vincent could only smile to suppress the acidic feeling rising in his chest. "I'm still failing to connect the dots."

"Is Lenoir home?" Oz asked.

"She is not. She's at a friend's. If you have daughters, then you know how they cannot be in one place for very long, especially at this age."

"That is quite true," he nodded.

"What may I ask do you want with Lenoir?"

"I want to ask her about her travels. She's been away for a long time, yes?"

"She's been back for a bit of time too."

"From overseas?"

"Yes," Vincent nodded. "Again, daughters want to roam. But Lenoir," he laughed nervously, "Well let's just say I can be thankful she was born with legs rather than wheels."

The man smiled politely, but it was clear he didn't care for – what was it supposed to be? A stall tactic? A joke? *What are you doing Vincent? Tell him, he may be able to help you.*

Vincent stammered when this voice screamed at him.

"I beg your pardon?" Oz asked.

He was at a loss and the hole he was sinking into was only getting deeper. What kind of father turns in his own daughter? You don't stab family in the back, you save them. The whole situation, the whole having to protect her act, felt oddly familiar to Vincent, but he could not place the feeling. It was lost in a sea of memories.

He cleared his throat and finally answered his question a second time, "Yes, from Overseas."

"Any idea what compelled her to travel so far away from home?"

Vincent chuckled; his insides actually relaxed a bit.

"Something funny?"

"I'm trying to figure out how to explain Lenoir to someone who doesn't know her. It's no easy feat."

"Try me," he folded his arms, ruffling his cheap suit.

"You can't exactly pinpoint or predict where she will go next or what she will do, but you can always trust Lenoir to be Lenoir," he explained.

"Is that a creative way of telling me she does what she wants."

"She does what she thinks is best. Always. I have no doubt my daughter has always been sincere, but if her aim is off, you'd never know it. She is so convincing that you almost believe it."

Oz raised an eyebrow.

"Even though it may sound like it, I'm not calling my daughter a liar. Absolutely not, no – she believes it herself, that's what makes it so convincing."

"So, she wanted to travel the world?"

"Yes, she's always had a bug for adventure. When she was one, I was driving home one day early from work, and there she was walking down Alta Avenue. No shirt, no shoes, wearing only a diaper. She had somehow slinked out of my wife's arms when she took her down for a nap, climbed out a window, somehow got out of the security gate and took off." Vincent smiled as he remembered, but it also brought with it the familiar feeling of not having any semblance of control over Lenoir. A pain that has since been renewed. "By the time she got to high school she had shunned almost everything we had. We aren't as well off as we were then, but she was always ashamed of our wealth. The fact that we had it better than so many others. She was always insistent on shopping at the Salvation Army, buying Junkers from friends before I could help her pick out a car. All the privilege that came with it, she wanted nothing to do with. She couldn't wait to shed it – in some ways to shed us as well I suppose. You know what it's like when you are young. You get the itch, that's what my father-in-law used to call it anyway. I suppose that is why Lenoir went off on her own."

"Did you ever worry she would not return? Or for her safety?"

"I did, in the beginning. I also knew if I continued to worry it would drive me crazy. Plus, I had Piper to take care of, and I was building my business. I didn't always worry about her, but I always knew she would be safe. Or that she could at least take care of herself."

"What about after 9/11? Did you worry then?"

"Of course I did," Vincent heard a slight irritation in his own voice.

There was a long silence as Oz wrote down something in chicken scratch on his note pad. Vincent craned his neck to see if he could make anything out, but Oz reacted as if he knew Vincent would look and tilted his pad out of view.

It took such a long while for Oz to review his thoughts that Vincent's own mind drifted on the wind. He took in the sounds of his environment, gazing wearily at the Spring sun. It was warm, even for California in March. The winter rains had not come like they ought to, the Whimbrels stuck around stubbornly circling him and Oz like vultures waiting for death. The sound of the sea foam washing ashore from blocks away eclipsed the scratching of Oz's notepad. Somebody hollered out on Ocean Avenue for another to pick up an extra hot dago.

Finally, Oz asked his next inevitable question, "So what do you think it was that Lenoir got into while she was over there?"

"What makes you think I think she got into anything?" Vincent asked defensively, his stomach in knots.

"Come now, Mr. Adams. I was just in your kitchen. Despite your attempt to shield me from your research, I know exactly what is going on. I feel for you. I don't know what I would do in your place. Like I said, I have daughters

[135]

too. For your benefit, I will not feign ignorance. But we both know your daughter may have gotten mixed up with the wrong crowd. A group whose name you may now very well know. So why can't we just cut through it and figure out the best way to help Lenoir? Hmm?"

Vincent, stunned on the inside managed to portray a look of bewilderment on the outside. "Okay, now you've lost me."

Oz sighed and dug out a wad of folded up paper from the pocket of his trousers. He unfolded it untidily, not exactly a trait Vincent expected from a man who seemed so structured and deliberate. "Here Mr. Adams," he held out the paper for him to take.

"Call me Vincent," he folded his arms.

"Take it. You want to know, don't you? Isn't this what you have been working so hard toward lately?" He waved the paper in front of him. The first page had text, some of which was highlighted, other lines were completely blacked out.

Vincent displayed a look of bemusement, "And what exactly is this?"

"Only one way to find out," Oz patiently held the documents in front of him.

He took it and started reading the first few lines of text, some kind of deposition, the deposed name was Franco Mahmid. One section jumped out at him right away, it confirmed Vincent's worst fears and solidified his suspicions all in one gut wrenching turn. Highlighted was the name "The People's Eternal Light."

Vincent, however, did not have time to react. He felt the watchful eye of the agency man beside him as he skimmed the rest of the words. They became discombobulated on the page and jumbled up into nonsensical gibberish by the time they reached his brain. His mind was somewhere else, his thoughts raced on the wind along with the Whimbrels. If Oz knows about the

People's Light, then of course he's after her. *You saw his shield,* his mind reasoned again, *what do you expect would happen if you turn her over?*

It angered Vincent. For the first time in his adult life his anger boiled over into a sea of red. All this talk about helping Lenoir before it's too late. He'd be helping her right into a secret CIA prison where she would vanish overseas once more, only this time she would never be heard from again. *Maybe,* another voice contradicted, *or maybe you have just read one too many Tom Clancy novels in your day.*

"Turn the page," Oz coaxed.

On the next page was a picture inside a low-lit temple of some kind. Featured were several men and women in white robes, sitting in a circle. The people were made up of all shapes, sizes and colors, making it nearly impossible to guess where the picture might have been taken. There were two Japanese men who looked like twins sitting next to one another in the lotus position, one had his eyes half shut looking like he was in an eternal state of bliss. The other looked contemplatively toward the camera, taking in the lens as if he had never seen a thing like it. Next to them was an Indian girl who wore a white veil atop of her head. No bindi was present on her forehead, she wore no makeup and was looking at something off camera. She held the hand of a tall, Danish looking girl next to her. She wore no veil, and her hair was cropped in a short tomboyish bowl cut. Laying his head on her lap was another dark-skinned fellow, skinny as a rail. He wore thin rimmed glasses that fit neatly over his head, he looked up at the camera dreamily. Torches or pyres were lit in the background of this photograph, focusing the uneven light. Shadows eclipsed the faces of all in the photo. But something else stood out to Vincent. The style of dress. He could almost swear he had seen one of those robes before, but where?!

"Recognize anyone?" Oz asked eventually.

"Should I?" Vincent kept it light, an awkward smile on his face.

"You wonder what this motley crew might be so happy about though, don't you?"

"Looks like a hippy commune to me. Maybe they're on drugs?" Vincent pitched his voice to make it sound like he was guessing.

"Take a look at the next one."

Vincent flipped to the next page which featured the same group of people, with several more white robes in the background standing over what looked like a stone hearth, but it was being treated religiously, like an altar or a tabernacle. Every one of this photo's participants were all smiles, seeming proud of themselves and one another. He could only make out their heads as their bodies were intertwined and lost in a sea of white. He focused so much on the robes and where he may have seen them before, the used cloth look of the fabric, the drawstrings with their Victorian curtain presence, that he failed to notice what was lying upon the stone beneath the smiling faces. There, laid out, was a boy of thirteen—maybe twelve-- he was dark skinned and frail. His body was twisted up and there was blood running down his face, an opening was made somewhere near the top of his head, but Vincent couldn't tell where exactly.

He scoffed and flipped to the next picture. It was again the same group, this time they were all sitting in a circle, the altar and the frail, bloody boy behind them. Sitting in the middle of the circle was an older man, the Jesus to his disciples. He had a long gray braid running down his back, but the rest of his head was tucked underneath the same kind of white hood some of the others wore.

"Meet Isik Veren," Oz narrated.

"He's the leader I take it," Vincent was no longer able to inject any sense of humor into his responses.

He flipped to the next photo and the whole group was in some kind of ceremony or dance. It was a wider shot, detailing the scope of the pack they ran with. There were maybe a hundred people in all, Africans, Arabs, Jews, South Asians, Europeans, it did not seem to matter. There were men intertwined with women, children in smaller sized robes. A newborn nursing at their mother's breast. Elders with gold trim lining their tattered robes watched the crowd perform their heretical dance. The full shrine was in the photo and indeed there were two large pyres symmetrically on both sides. Other bodies of destitute looking peasants were on the stairs leading up the altar. Some seemed to move within the photograph. All looked on with a terror Vincent thought he recognized. Not that the worry he had over his daughter could match whatever pain they were going through. The white robes danced and smiled as the tortured looked on. Then he could feel it. Last night's whiskey bath was at the back of his throat, knocking on the door of the ether, begging to be let out.

Vincent swallowed to supplant it, "Why are you showing me these?"

"I'm showing you what they are capable of," Oz retorted. "These people are here, Mr. Adams, in California. They came back with her. You must have seen them. Go back to the other pages. Take a good look. You must have seen something."

Vincent shook his head in an attempt to rid himself of the ringing that turned his brains to mush. "I- I don't know what to say."

"Say you want to help your daughter."

"I don't know what to do."

"Bring her to me, Vincent. It's not too late for her. She can help us make sure something like this never happens again." He pointed to the altar and the bloodied fragile boy strewn across it.

[139]

"My DAUGHTER!" Vincent cried. He froze with Oz watching him intently. He counted to five and took deep breaths. He refused to lose it in front of the agency man. He could not betray his daughter. Something inside told him he could solve this on his own. He didn't need this Oz fellow to assist him. "Has nothing to do with this," he shoved the wad of paper back to Oz.

Frustrated, the agency man folded them back up as sloppily as he took them out. "It's not like there haven't been signs in the past, though, am I right Vincent?"

Still shaken, he hardly registered what was said. A sudden urgency welled up within Vincent, and he wanted nothing more but to talk to Lenoir again. He cursed himself for letting this go on as long as he had.

Oz stood up, stretching his legs and back. "You know I thought I would do you the courtesy of visiting first. But we will get Lenoir, one way or another. Thanks to this new legislation, I can get all the evidence I need. I can get a warrant. But after that it will be too late. The world doesn't want to harbor terrorists, Vincent. Even if you do."

"You're lying."

"Am I? Does your daughter have a cell phone? Does she go online?" he smiled, "Of course she does, all kids do now."

"Apparently you weren't listening very closely to what I said before," Vincent managed a sickly smile underneath all the pain. "Lenoir shunned those kinds of privileges long ago."

"I guess these feelings have been festering for a while. That explains a lot. Thank you for your time, Vincent."

"Call me Mr. Adams," he called after him sarcastically.

Quiet enveloped Vincent after that. He sat glued to his seat for a while after the agency man dropped the bomb

[140]

on him. He sat watching the sky. The occasional white puff devolved into a gray smattering of paint splashes. The dark seemed to be overtaking the light in front of him, one moment at a time. It seemed his whole life was trending this way. After all, what had he been doing these last few months? Trying to save his daughter is what.

And what was it this Oz fellow was offering you – for Lenoir.

Not a chance at redemption, he shook his head. There is nothing redeeming about sitting in an island prison cell for the rest of one's life, being harassed or worse by whatever college dropout they hire to guard it. Besides, simply talking to people was not a crime – was it? Lenoir had done nothing wrong. She would never hurt anyone. Isn't that true? Hasn't that always been true?

But it hadn't – had it?

Vincent had blocked it out of his mind the moment he heard the words himself, trying to bury it as deep as it would go. He had always chosen to remember Lenoir on his own terms. Hell, it probably directly influenced her own stubbornness. Nevertheless, slowly this distorted feeling came back to him. One memory at a time.

As he remembered, he absent-mindedly bolted the door of his kitchen from the outside. His body seemed to operate on some kind of preternatural instinct, going through the motions while his mind raced back in time. Going faster and faster as he marched alongside the house, around the old, crumbling fountain that Pamela so cherished but hadn't been hooked up to a water pipe in years. The time he thought about was the only time a school administrator had ever phoned him about Lenoir. Sure, he thought, as he started his car and squealed his tires down the drive, he had received many kind comments at parent/teacher conferences, but this call was about something else.

Lenoir was on the honor roll all throughout high school and was the co-valedictorian at graduation. However, the one dark blemish on her permanent record, as school officials love to call it, was there, however microscopic.

As Vincent turned onto Palms Boulevard, he realized that no matter how hard he tried, there was no denying this incident happened. It made him think about how poorly he reacted, by ignoring it in hopes it would go away. And in a way, it had. He remembered something else too, as he took a route once very familiar, but now a faded memory. He remembered how he felt when he was called into that meeting, how wounded, confused and how he had wished Pamela were still alive because she would know exactly what to do. *Any of those feelings feel familiar?* That sardonic voice asked him again. "This time is different," he said aloud whilst driving.

How so?

"This could mean her life."

As he thought about this, the photos the investigator showed him flashed through his mind. The curled up bloodied boy that lay like a broken ball of twine on the stone slab. The smiling faces that surrounded him. More third-world poor strewn about and festooned as if they were decorations for some deviant ceremony. *There is just no way Lenoir would be a part of something like that.* If there was one thing he knew about his daughter, and knew it still to be true, there is not a dishonorable bone in her body. She was always doing what she thought was right, and not right for her, but right for everyone else. Even if what she was doing was wrong. She was always so focused in on the cause that she often never saw the big picture. He couldn't fault her for that, and that may have been where he'd led her astray.

He arrived at what used to be known as the third place. That was what he and his friends called it. They had their home lives, which was one, they had the university and they had the Viaduct that overlooked one of the more scenic areas of the Los Angeles River. The bridge was only 1500 feet long give or take, but enough to feel segregated from the city, if only for a little bit.

The area had gone to hell in the last several decades but when he and his buddies loaded up whoever's vehicle was available with cases of Ballantine and hoofed it up to the bridge, they would hang out for hours. No one bothered them. They would spend the night seeing who could hit which plank off the side of the bridge with their dead soldiers and bank it onto an adjacent target. All while discussing which sorority had the best-looking girls or what guilt trip their old man had laid on them. Today, kids are expected to go to college, back then it was considered a luxury. From the neighborhoods that some of his classmates were from, it might even be considered a slight to those who did not have the funding or wherewithal to go.

Vincent parked near the north bank of the river and climbed a set of access stairs. A few things had changed. The bridge was an off-color white now, back then it was baby blue. When he got to the top, he realized they had added several more lanes of traffic. The same view of downtown though. The skyline looked moralistic in the midst of the gloomy sky and the thoughts racing through his head.

Once he settled into his old spot, he looked down to scout for any empty cans of Ballantine, but of course, there were none. The Los Angeles department of corrections had to stay in business somehow. There were truckloads of trash to cleanup along the banks of the river of angels. He sat down on the walkway and stuck his legs through the deck railings, the grating wrinkling his ass. He looked down at the river; it was eerily calm and not the wimpy trickle that can be seen throughout the waterways of most of the city. He thought about another gray day. A day not that far from memory, yet he had to travel far to unearth it.

It was six years ago. Lenoir was a sophomore. An unexpected phone call had taken him away from work. He remembered finding it whimsical that Lenoir would be in trouble for anything. *What'd she do? Let someone cheat off her paper?* He remembered asking the school secretary.

"I'm afraid it is a little more serious than that," she led him toward the principal's office while motioning for Lenoir to stay put outside, all in one graceful movement. He remembered being impressed that she was able to sit her down so easily without getting a word back in return.

Once he took his seat in the office, the principal, a rotund man who looked like he took everything in life excessively seriously, stared at him behind thick square frames. Vincent looked around the man's office, a smattering of teaching accolades and letters from the school board commending him on his service were littered throughout. When it became apparent that the man was waiting for Vincent to speak, he piped up, "So, you had something to tell me about my daughter?"

"Yes," the man licked his finger in order to thumb through Lenoir's file, which was as thin as the manila folder it sat in. "She exhibited some inappropriate behavior today that has us concerned."

"Oh?" Vincent, still tickled by the dire face he wore, couldn't understand what his daughter could do to provoke such a reaction.
"Does that surprise you?"

"A little bit," Vincent laughed nervously. "I mean, I've never had any trouble with her in the past, and I'm pretty sure you haven't either."

"While it's true she has no history of behavior problems-" he paused, reading one of the only pieces of paper in Lenoir's file.

[144]

"Yes?" Vincent waited for the rest. The man was beginning to get on his nerves. He was talking about Lenoir as if she were a common hooligan that graced his office every other day.

"The seriousness of this incident has us concerned."

Vincent folded his arms, "Are you going to tell me what she did?"

He cleared his throat, "To put it simply, Mr. Adams. She threatened a school official. My vice principal in fact. He is Lenoir's track coach."

"Ah yes, Mr. Trunchbull. She threatened him? How, exactly? With getting a letter in track?"

The principal remained humorless, "Quite simply, she said she was going to poison his daughter, who I may add Mr. Adams, is a vulnerable child with physical and mental issues. Not very nice, wouldn't you say?"

Vincent shook his head. "Did you hear this firsthand?"

"Mr. Trunchbull informed me of it."

"And you believe it? Do you know Lenoir at all?"

"No, Mr. Adams, I don't. But I do know my vice principal and I believe him when he says it."

"Is he here?" Vincent looked around as if he were going to magically appear.

"No, he's gone home for the day."

"Well, he knows Lenoir. And I want to hear the exact circumstances in which this threat was uttered. Have you even asked her about it?"

The man took off his thick glasses and nodded, "Mr. Adams, Lenoir has admitted to making the threat."

He paused, not sure if he heard him right. "Come again?"

"I said, your daughter has confirmed she made the threat."

"That's impossible," he took another breath. "Why aren't we asking her about this? Why isn't she in here too?"

"In due time Mr. Adams, I wanted to speak with you first privately."

"It's got to be a joke or a misunderstanding. Lenoir, she's not violent, she's too smart to make a comment like that, and she knows it's wrong."

"Nevertheless," the principal said smugly, holding up an open hand.

Vincent narrowed his eyes; he was starting to get the feeling that the man thought he was a bad parent. True, he had been busy building his career at the firm, but the conversation and the circumstances of him being there had completely blindsided him. He figured there had to have been a missing piece that would clear everything up.

"I want to tell you what is going to happen, Mr. Adams. My vice principal was very shaken up by this comment. As you can imagine since you have daughters, it was quite disturbing. I asked him what he thinks should happen to remedy this situation."

"Okay," Vincent folded his hands suddenly feeling very embarrassed about the whole thing. "So, she's suspended, right?"

"Well yes, but I'm afraid there is more to it than that. When violence is incited or even mentioned on school property, it is our policy to call the police."

"She's just a kid," it came out as a whisper.

"She is, Mr. Adams. Someday she will be an adult."

"Don't you think this is going overboard just a little bit?"

"I've reviewed the situation with the super intendent and even if Mr. Trunchbull is not going to press charges, the district will have to. We wanted to pay you the courtesy of knowing first. Now, seeing that Lenoir's a juvenile, they will most certainly release her into your custody. But Mr. Adams, we are looking at a two-week suspension and she will also be prohibited from remaining on with the track team."

[146]

Vincent let out a sigh. Here he thought the trip down here would be for something stupid. That Lenoir had stolen a piece of school memorabilia, or she cussed out a teacher, not this—not *his* daughter. Not *Pamela's* daughter. How he wished she were there. She seemed to have been clued in on the fact somehow when the girls were young just how much trouble daughters could bring. He wished she had told him.

By the time the excruciating, humiliating conversation with the principal ended, Vincent exited his office just in time to see the arresting officer placing the cuffs on Lenoir. He seemed to be making a big show of it. The officer, a big burly Irish guy, was in full "bad cop" mode. He probably thought Lenoir was a constantly troubled student who needed to be scared straight. At that moment, Vincent was no longer certain that it wasn't true.

Of course, Lenoir being Lenoir, never gave them the satisfaction of looking scared. In fact, as she was being led away with half of the administration office looking on, she hesitated to show any emotion at all. Her blue eyes seemed to conform to the situation as if she had been in it hundreds of times before. As if she were that troubled student the principal and the officer were making her out to be. That, in effect, was the most troubling thing of all.

Instead of telling her it would be okay, or that he would be right down to the station to get her, the look on her face froze him in his tracks. Vincent probably looked more helpless than she did, almost as if he were the one in the cuffs.

Vincent stared down at the water, leaning his head against a bridge truss remembering the situation. Of course, Lenoir had a reason, and a strong one at that like he knew she would. Apparently, a friend of hers had been tardy to a study hall one too many times and was in danger of being kicked off track. Lenoir being the altruistic, freedom fighter she thought she was went to go plead her friend's case. Apparently, unbeknownst to Lenoir (the principal had filled him in), Mr. Trunchbull's father had passed away earlier that afternoon and he was in no mood to debate with Lenoir. Things got heated and she had said what she said.

Later at home he confronted her about it. He didn't even remember what she had said, but he could not forget the look on her face, this unassuming, blasé look as if they had been discussing what to have for dinner, and the unconcerned way she addressed her own actions. It didn't occur to Vincent until that moment, but it was the reason he had buried it so deep. That penetrating look she got in her eye when he knew there was no way he could change her mind or talk her out of it. She was so very willful, and it made him feel helpless.

He thought about the principal, the conversation. Maybe he didn't take it seriously enough. Maybe he was glossing over his lack of parenting. Maybe sometime after Pamela died, Lenoir desperately needed guidance in something he had failed to provide. The list and what ifs could go on and on, but it certainly didn't make him feel better. The principal was trying to offer him help, Vincent either was too preoccupied or simply failed to see the lifeline he was being tossed.

And here he was again with history repeating itself. Would Vincent grab the lifeline this time before it was too late? He was given more than his share of information to make the decision, yet he still felt trapped.

Of course, the agency man was attempting to manipulate him, but he didn't lie to him. He gave him valid information. How could he use it? Why did it feel like a piece of this was still missing? Then as his foot lifted up and hovered over the edge, he thought about the madness of their dress. The white robes. The cloth that looked so pure and innocent. Maybe it meant something or maybe it meant nothing at all.

Vincent thought about Piper, how ignored she must have felt throughout this ordeal. Was he making the same mistakes all over again? Was he a neglectful father?

His foot hovered still in midair. He thought about what might happen if he took one more step, folding himself over the bridge truss and tossing himself into the River of Angels. Becoming an angel seemed like the less stressful option than pursuing this path. How could he not fail her now when he had done it so many times before? All the memories flashed back to him: the night he hadn't realized she had been out until three am at sixteen years old, the time he almost let her drown in the university pool, and the moment he realized he had left her at the Century Square Shopping Center, two hours after he had gotten home.

The last one caused him to misstep, his right arm came up so violently on the metal tress that he had ripped open the side of his hand. All that stood between him and the water was his strength in that hand. He looked at it as the blood trickled down his palm and dripped off onto the walkway. The sun had gone all the way down and the lamps lighting the viaduct bridge shined hazily on them like a lighthouse on the shore of some desolate beach. The lamps set along the bottom deck of the bridge seemed to overtake him, driving thoughts of darkness further into the corners of his mind.

One more step, his mind told him, *and it could all be over.*

At home, he felt no better. The gravity of the situation, as well as the ideas planted by the agency man had weighed heavy on his mind. It was like that for days. Even the new information presented to him didn't seem worth looking into. He was rung up, defeated. There was nowhere to go. If he had stepped off the bridge, nothing in the last few days would have been any different. It only seemed prudent to sit on the couch and wait for the agency man and his bullies to kick the door down so he could watch his daughter be hauled off again in cuffs with that same blank look on her face.

One evening during a marathon of mind-numbing reruns on Nick at Nite, a night like those before it. A night that saw Vincent's stubble turn a sour gray and the patches of hair he slept on stay fixed in their chaotic shapes; Lenoir walked in. He had neither seen nor heard her. She had just suddenly appeared in front of an episode of MASH, which he had not been watching either. He was looking at something beyond the screen, lost in a tunnel of more of that darkness. When she popped into his view, the screen on the television faded to white and the whole room was bathed in pure, ashen light, he was sure the fluorescent tube inside had popped. But the commercial break came on and the low din of the flickering screen returned the room to the glib shadows.

She was standing in front of him with her arms folded, she was looking at him quizzically in her ever-present patience. When she stared for more than her share of a few seconds, he realized she was waiting for a reply. "What?" the sound of television static hissed in his ears until he could bring his focus entirely back to her.

"It's three AM, what are you still doing up?"

"Oh," he sat up and his neck barked at him for the uncomfortable position he had left it in for so long, "I must have fallen asleep."

Her expression did not change, "You weren't asleep."

"Well, maybe I should go," he muttered, hardly even able to look at her. Every time he looked her in the eyes, it recalled his failures.

"That's probably a good idea," she moved silently up the stairs without looking back.

He looked around helplessly before locating the remote, pressing the button and turning the den into a black hole. The shadows from the sycamore tree outside the window seemed to goad him into action.

When he was at her bedroom door, he almost knocked, but the shadows sparking this maneuver kept at him and instead he walked in.

"Dad!" she hissed. "What if I had been changing?"

He blinked, willing himself to stay out of that tunnel. That tediously, colorless tunnel where light can't escape.

Light

She was halfway into a crossed legged pose on her bed when he had come in. Prepared before her neatly on the covers were an almost burned down candle, a hand mirror that he recognized as her grandmother's, a photo of a man in a white

Light

robe, and a leather-bound book with no art or distinguishing marks on the cover. It looked like she was either about to perform some kind of ritual or shoot up.

He ignored her perfectly reasonable comment and grabbed the photo from the tray she had her items placed on. It was an elderly man who looked like he had not bathed in a week. He had dirt caked over his face, his hair was long and greasy, and his beard was salt and peppered with fungus. An open sore festered on his cheek. He had one eye halfway open as the flash bulb on the camera captured his image. "Is this him?" he waved the picture at her.

For a moment, it almost looked as if she would cry. That this shadow had pushed him too far, that the energy it provided had not been distributed equitably.

He took a breath and a half a step back when her face changed completely.

She didn't seem hurt by his comment at all, instead she used it. She smiled that same lofty smile and replied, "This is Isik Veren."

[151]

Vincent sneered at the photo, now that a name could be given to the face. "And who is he to you?"

The smile evaporated and her looked turned more thoughtful. "He's the giver of light."

Vincent held himself back all the more. He steeled himself, waiting for another onslaught of emotions to pass. "He's- Does that mean he protects you?"

"He does many things, but protection is not one of them. The light protects us."

"Do you love him?"

"Of course."

"Are you-" he didn't know how to ask. The dull throbbing of the last what- several weeks? Months? Had been replaced by a fresh wound. He couldn't place it because that tunnel was starting to call him back. "Are you special to him? Or is there more than one?"

"It's not like that," she grinned sheepishly. "I'm not sleeping with hi-"

"That's not what I was asking."

"Then what?"

"Huh?"

"What were you asking?"

"I want to know! That's all. I want to know," he sucked a thin stream of air between his teeth, forcing himself to slow down. To plan the next step before it got all twisted up again. "I want to know who has held my girl's attention these last few years. I want to know if you're okay. I mean – I want to know if he is who your spending time with that he's treating you right. I have that right you know. I'm your father," he tried to manage a grimace.

Lenoir smiled though. She smiled deeply. She took hold and embraced him. "Listen to me, you will always be my father." She let go as he fumbled with a small tear from one corner of his face.

"Just hearing that makes me feel a ton better," he laughed, but the shadow grew taller.

[152]

"You know, I was about to call to the light if you want to join me," she regarded her items on the tray.

He looked at her and it was like taking the first step off a sandbar in the middle of the ocean, feeling the depth and cold darkness beneath you. He ignored her invitation and pressed on, "Boy, I'm so happy for you. I really am. I'd sure like to meet this Isik fellow that makes you so happy."

She smiled patiently, looking years older at that moment. " That's not really how it works."

"Why not?" he grinned.

"Because Isik's not here."

"Well, of course he's not *here*, but we could arrange for some kind of social engagement," he kidded.

"I don't believe you would be ready to go that far."

"Honey—I visited you, didn't I? They have these things called airplanes." The depth grew like a black hole.

"Oh dad," she said sadly.

"What?" he whispered, running out of breath.

"You're in such pain."

He nodded slowly, holding off another burst rising up from the depth below the tunnel. "I'm glad you've noticed. You've probably been seeing that look more and more recently." His head continued to bob. He was either still nodding or shaking uncontrollably—he could not decipher which.

She stared at him. The walls of her face were an impenetrable fortress that was locked up like one hundred Fort Knox's. She wasn't angry, she wasn't vengeful or upset. She didn't come back with a snide remark or a hurt look or any of those things other daughters might do. She only studied. She eyed the photo of Isik Veren still in his hand. Shaking along with the rest of him.

"Do you have anything to say about any of that pain. Mine or others?" he asked desperately, afraid of the answer.

"Just this: this is my home, and you are my father. It is something not even the light can change. No one can. It

[153]

just is. And Svarga kē rājya is Svarga kē rājya, and Isik is Isik. You are unable to change that. I want it. That is what I'm trying to say. I will do anything to get in."

"In? In where?"

"Into Svarga kē rājya."

"Translate please."

"The Kingdom of Heaven."

He looked upon her helplessly. "We've gone to church. I brought you when you were younger."

"Mother brought us."

"We *both* did," he paused. "You know I went a little bit after she died."

"You did?"

He nodded.

"Why never an invite?"

"I don't know. I was ashamed I think."

"Why would you ever be ashamed of your faith?"

"Aren't you the least bit ashamed of your light?"

"I'm not," she smiled again. "It brings me the complete opposite."

He hardly had the energy to look at her any longer. All that sitting on the sofa, lost in his tunnel. How long had it even been?

"So," she started. "You've asked me all kinds of questions. I've answered them all truthfully. I have no reason to lie to you. I would tell you anything you wanted to know. But I wonder, if I were to ask you some questions. Would you tell me honestly? Would you lie to me to protect me in that paternal manner? Would you keep something from me?"

"Ask me anything Lenoir."

"There are many questions I've always wanted to ask you."

"Pick one."

"The only one that comes to mind is also the most important."

"Ask it," he tensed.

"Why couldn't you save it?"

"What?"

"All of it. Mom, us. God? Why won't you save you? It hurts me. You don't understand. It's like I'm screaming to a crowd full of people and everyone is ignoring me. Then I have to call out and whisper goodbye. Goodbye."

His eyes had closed somewhere along the line. Inside them an ocean of anguish was swelling up, waiting to boil over. He had several thoughts, but none could escape.

"You see now, don't you?" she prided herself. "That's how the dark parts of the world operate. There's no secrets in the light. There's none of this."

He regarded her. Thinking there was probably no way to grab hold of it. It's like a disease. He *did* see that now. Four years she had been away. He doesn't know how many years she had lived with it, but it could be embedded too deeply now. He could think of only one thing to tell her. She was his daughter after all. He had to warn her. The agent who had visited him, Oz.

"Your silence speaks more than words could. You could come with me," she looked genuinely excited at the idea.

"No," he took a step back. "No, it's not right." He cleared his throat. "College I mean. You have to pick a college, okay? Just think about it huh?" His words choked something and suddenly the spark was snuffed out. "You know, I think I'm too tired to continue this conversation right now. But I would like to talk about college soon."

"Yes," she nodded. "You're right. It's time to start getting prepared."

"For now, I'm going to go to bed."

He turned to leave and was back out in the hall.

"Rest well dad," her mechanical response seemed to kick back into gear, and it was as if he hadn't reached her on any level at all. Her emotional EKG was looking like doomsday, flat and lonely.

Part 7

It's Not Enough, So I'll Just Say Goodbye

So, where are you?

More importantly, where were you? Have you found your way back to us? This time, we can only hope it is forever. We chose you for a reason. You may have mistakenly thought you chose us, but your confidence makes you transparent in your projected shortcomings. Remember that Isik sees you, is always with you and always loves you. Even during these times of trial for control over one's own life.

You have struggled, as we all have.

So confident were you on your return to your homeland, but the roots you broke free of have restored. The most painful part is behind you. Soon you will be with your guardians once more. Soon you will be in the rājya, the seraphs will celebrate your contribution in helping the world back to its feet. To make them all see that the light is not the end but merely a beginning. We find ourselves in transition along with you, a door you will help open.

Soon after, Isik will rejoin you and he will be yours, as you will be his. They chose you for a reason, *hamaare peele sipaahee*. Anyone of Isik's brethren could have been selected, but he knew you were the one from the moment you wandered into Makaan. This selection goes far greater than your external beauty and strong convictions but are more in line with the tools needed to serve the light in this capacity.

Strong you are, beautiful too, but these attributes will only bring you so far in the dark corners of the world. They will serve not in the light. The time for doubt has passed, the time for action is close at hand. Your guardians will be in contact with you to help carry out your contribution. After, the clout and inspiration, the mere mention of your name, will carry with it courage and faith.

Isik compels you to finish what you started. The guardians will take care of your logistics, all you must do is repel the darkness. Those from your homeland will request you stay – implore you even – but alas, your resolve will prevail over their obscure desires. Rely on your internal fire and that of your companions. Bring any of those ready to receive the light, but do not be fooled by their false determination in extracting you from it.

We have come too far and carry too significant a message to become befuddled in the material world. Remember Isik's teachings that *love is the answer for both the light and the dark. It shines brightly upon you in the hour of your greatest need if you allow it that- but can also illuminate your way out of the twisted passages of doubt and self-loathing. While none of us can penetrate those passages at the current – someday a savior will walk among us with angelic hair and the face of 'eardh. She will bring Isik's teachings to the west and convey our message of contribution and love while sacrificing everything – for us. *

They ask you about the man in trouble. The one who comes from the same deprivation as you. His failure will highlight your success. Isik compels you to lean on his teachings and speak them with your fellow guardians. After all, it was his words that met your cries even before he spoke them to you. *Let all men share in the responsibility that birthed our current realm to not only exist, but to decay, and allow all women the space and support to heal it.*

*From Section 145, unit 17 of the *Teachings of Isik**

Scarlett twisted a piece of her hair, wrapping it around her finger as she scanned the aisles of the *Mystical Moon*. The shelves were cluttered, but left plenty of space between crystals, bags of minerals and rocks that cure depression, essential oil potions that cast influence over your body and soul and scented candles that brought about good luck.

The next aisle was stacked to the ceiling with books from different periods, some leather-bound, others spiral, and some had golden gilded edges on the tops of their pages like a bible. She found Lenoir in this aisle, thumbing through a pamphlet that included a local map of places deemed worthy to worship.

"Hey girl!" Scarlett strode up to give her a hug.

Surprisingly, Lenoir dodged it without looking up. "Listen to this, 'Why don't witches have temples? We don't feel the need for a place that is set aside from daily life. To many Wiccans, that wouldn't seem right, since Wicca is firmly rooted in the Earth. We like to see and smell and hear and feel and even taste the Divine all around us.' Isn't that a bit contradictory?"

"What is?" Scarlett wondered, confused.

"They say they can worship anywhere, but then go on to explain that worship must be in a place where you 'taste sea breeze, can gather earth in your hand where you sit and smell at least two different variations of fauna.' That's pretty limiting. Silly. The light teaches us that even the deepest, darkest cave can be your temple and that the light within will eclipse any darkness if that's where you choose to practice."

A woman appeared beside them, she wore a second-hand crumpled dress with a frilly midriff and a long skirt. Braids appeared in her matted hair; she smiled as her nose ring gleamed in the afternoon light. "If you'd like to learn more, you could join us at one of our workshops on Mondays at 5."

Scarlett smirked and looked to Lenoir. They used to visit this shop in high school. Scarlett didn't give a damn about the religion but liked some of the decorative knick-knacks and symbols. Even though she found the *one with the earth* philosophy simple and outdated, there was also a part of her that liked the communal measure of the Wiccan faith. It gave her hope of a sense of belonging in a world where it was tough to find a place to belong. She picked it to start their afternoon of shopping because it was a place both familiar and comforting.

"We are just browsing, thanks," Lenoir returned her smile.

"If you need anything, or have any questions please communicate." she swayed in the opposite direction, moving breezily in her long skirt.

Scarlett arched her eyebrows, but returned to face Lenoir, who was already looking at her.

"Hi," she said it like she would to a child.

"Hey. Can I get my hug now or are you that averse to touch?" Scarlett chided her.

Lenoir, who she noticed dressed in similar fashion to the Wiccans, looked like she could belong anywhere she wanted. She threw her arms around her friend as they embraced in the middle of all the pagan textbooks and writings on how to summon your spirit guide. "This was a wonderful idea, thank you for inviting me," she crooned.

"When was the last time me and my girl were able to go shopping, just the two of us? You remember our Saturdays in 11th grade?"

"Oh god," Lenoir pulled back from her "we were inseparable there for a while. I still don't know where you got the money for half the stuff you bought."

"The two Bs, boyfriends and babysitting," Scarlett prided herself. "You hardly ever bought anything."

"I just liked to look. I preferred to obtain my items in other ways."

"Yeah, you don't have to tell me. So where are we headed after this, flower child? Or are we spending our whole afternoon on the moon?"

"I have a few places I need to stop for some supplies, but the world is ours. What shall we do with it?"

"Well," Scarlett began, "I was thinking we could look at the rest of this block and then cruise up to Market Street and check out some of the boutiques. What do you say?"

"Sounds wonderful, Scarlett. My stops are in between, would you want to walk?"

Scarlett paused and thought about the blisters she would be scrubbing off her feet later, but she wanted to have a nice afternoon with Lenoir. She had been feeling a bit separated from her friends lately. Sure, she had made plenty of new ones since high school, but they were all so exhausting and demanding, plus they all had a lot more money than Scarlett did. "A walk sounds nice," Scarlett agreed.

After exiting the Mystical Moon, they sauntered west, grabbing iced teas at a Starbucks on the way. Lenoir talked about school a bit, how she had applied to Stanford as well as a few backup colleges that Scarlett had never heard of. "You are not going to be leaving me so soon, are you?" she pretended to sound hurt.

A look of sadness crossed Lenoir's face, "Honey, believe me, I don't want to. But you know how it is. We all only have one life, and we have to make the most of it."

"Sigh," she shook her head.

After looking through a few shops, Scarlett started to feel better about her situation. It was like she and Lenoir had picked up right where they left off in 11th grade. As if no time had passed between then and now. She told her about a few of her most recent dates, including the trumpet player in a jazz trio named Bert who was old enough to be her father. "He had a sweet soul, but he smelled like garlic and cigars," Scarlett wrinkled her nose.

"Why did you go out with him in the first place?" Lenoir asked.

"My friend Macy made a bet with me that she could snag a musician before I did. It was a race and I lost...twice."

Lenoir laughed, "Oh to be young and in love."

"Something like that," Scarlett could laugh about it now, but getting rid of Bert was distressing at the time.

They started their walk to Market Street. The sun broke through the gloomy clouds and Scarlett had them stop at a *Sunglasses Hut* even though she had a pair buried somewhere deep in her purse. "You have to keep your eyes protected," she explained as she checked out her selections in the rotating mirrors. "If you don't, you are squinting, and the crow's feet come not long after that. Aren't you going to get a pair?"

"The light doesn't bother me. It fills me. If I get crow's feet, I get crow's feet."

"Impossible," Scarlett shook her head. "But if I had your skin tone, which is built better for aging, I probably wouldn't worry about it as much either. Thanks, mom, for the liver spots."

Lenoir laughed, "You don't have liver spots, and neither does your mom. You are two gorgeous women."

Scarlett reveled in the confidence boost. Lenoir had always been so positive to be around, she felt like everyone else was so empty in comparison. Her positivity was contagious, and Scarlett could store it for days after they hung out. It was just the thing she needed after such a rough year.

Once she settled on a cute pair of ginger colored keyhole bridges, they continued on their journey.

About halfway there, Lenoir suddenly changed directions eyeing the end of the block that contained a hardware store, a place to buy nurses uniforms and a *Hampton Inn.*

[164]

"It's a straighter shot if we keep on Lyons," Scarlett pointed out.

Lenoir, unfazed, maintained her direction, "This is one of my stops. It won't take very long, I promise."

She felt a wave of annoyance bubble up but remembered how great a shopping partner she had with her today. A big reason for that was her patience and willingness to follow Scarlett to the ends of the shopping earth without as much as a complaint. The least she could do is return the favor.

As they drew closer, Scarlett arched her pencil thin eyebrows above her new shades, "What, does a cute guy work here or something?"

Lenoir regarded her warmly, but then entered the neighborhood relic, the bell ringing as she stepped inside. Reluctantly, yet somehow curious – Scarlett followed.

The place smelled of wood chips and paint. There was definitely no hint of a cute man working the counter or stocking shelves. Only the same sweaty, geeky variety she had imagined. She laughed to herself as she imagined their talk of wrenches and drill bits, how simple and uncomplex their world was.

As Lenoir wandered off, she found the garden aisle and sorted through gnomes, gloves and flowerpots. She found a man in his thirties in the next aisle who looked a bit like Sean Faris. She batted her eyes at him as she passed, using her patented hair flip as he watched her go.

"Hey," he smiled at her.

"Why do they have so many varieties of brooms? Don't they all do the same thing?" Scarlett stared at the rows of brooms in amazement.

"Different bristles work better on different surfaces," he offered. "I don't think I've ever seen you here before."

"That's probably because it is my first time in here," she smiled.

"Can I get your number?" he asked, emboldened.

She smiled again, "How about I get yours instead?"

He hesitated, fidgeting with a couple of the items in his basket, some planks, a box of nails and something that looked to Scarlett like a wire clipper. When her eyes moved onto his broad shoulders and slowly made their way down his toned arms and up to his hands, she noticed his wedding band.

"Oh," she exclaimed without a hint of sultry left in her voice.

"Yeah," he said sheepishly, his face slightly red. "That's why it would be better to get your number."

She looked at him a moment more, rolled her eyes and stalked off to find Lenoir. "Too bad," she whispered to herself under her breath. She felt him peer around the corner of the aisle they had their moment in, watching her go.

"I think I just had my shortest relationship ever," she announced when she found Lenoir stacking large green bags of fertilizer into her cart.

"Oh yeah, did you get a name?" she asked as a couple of guys further down the aisle watched in amazement as this rail thin girl with skinny arms hefted 50lb bags into the cart without so much as a wince.

"What are you doing?" Scarlett paused her story to marvel along with the guys. "Are you making a garden?"

"That's as good an explanation I could tell you," she giggled strangely, eyeing the people gathered around and stopped at the fifth bag. "My dad asked me to get him this stuff."

Glancing uninterestedly over the other items in her cart, a fuel container and several large bags of cotton, Scarlett absent-mindedly asked, "How are you going to carry all this stuff around?"

"They deliver," she aimed a burst of strength at the cart to get it moving, breezing past the gawking men staring after her in disbelief.

"Anyway," Scarlett vied for her attention, "this dude has no qualms about hitting on me as he's practically stroking his wedding band. It's like, 'excuse me, what kind of Magdalene do you think I am?' Who do these guys think they are?"

"Some kind of elite breed of Lotharios I guess," Lenoir stared straight ahead, focused on something. As Scarlett was about to look up to see what it was, an outburst erupted from her usually even-keeled friend, "Oh no!"

"What's up?"

"I forgot the sawdust. Can you go and get a couple of bags for me and meet me up at the counter?"

"I wouldn't even know where to begin."

"Please? There's no way I could get this thing turned around with all this fertilizer," she tapped the cart with the toe of her shoe. "They are about this big," she held up her hands vertically, "just a couple of bags, regular old saw dust. Like you used to put in Bruno's cage, remember?"

"Sure," Scarlett hadn't thought about her childhood pet hamster in many years and was a bit astounded that Lenoir remembered, let alone his name. "But-"

"Thanks," Lenoir waved to her as she heaved herself against the cart to get it moving again, "you're the best!"

Scarlett watched her go, still not understanding the relevance of these supplies and the ease in which Lenoir pushed the cart that should be buckling under its own weight. "Trippy," she muttered to herself as she went off to search for the sawdust.

On her way she bumped into an older man who was distinguished looking, if not a bit dated in his dress. Her heart leapt right away at the thought of Bert returning to make another attempt to "woo her back" as he had put it. But it was someone else. He had been watching Lenoir as well, "Does your friend need help?" he looked concerned about something.

"Yes, but she would never accept it." How *do* you explain someone like Lenoir to a stranger, Scarlett thought. She might as well try and prepare caviar or run for city council. As she thought about other impossible tasks, she remembered the sawdust. She followed the smell of wood. The hardware store was crowded today, she passed several families, the married guy who refused her eye contact the second time around and a tall, serious looking guy with long hair who looked familiar. He was dressed in a white robe that sagged down to the floor, making it look like he was floating.

After several frustrating moments looking at the different types of sawdust, she threw off her new sunglasses in exasperation. While she was determined to complete this task for her friend, how was she supposed to know if Noir's dad wanted woodchips, wood particles or if he wanted dust from maple, ash or cottonwood. In the end, she settled on ash dust because it reminded her the most of what Bruno liked in his cage. She held out the bags in front of her as if a cockroach would come crawling out of them at any moment.

When she came to the front, there was a line of people, but no sign of Lenoir. Her cart full of fertilizer looked hastily pushed to the side and there were several staff members peering out the window facing the street. "Noir?" she called out, starting to get annoyed at this detour. If she wanted to waste time at a hardware store she could have gone with her stepdad and brother who were always wasting time out in the garage. "Noir?" she tried again without so much as anyone glancing in her direction. It gave her a sinking feeling. Scarlett had a reoccurring dream all the time of being in a large crowd of people calling out for someone to help, but everyone just ignoring her. People could be so cruel and dismissive if it didn't directly involve or benefit them in some way, and that stung her in a way she didn't even understand.

She started to become irritated, she threw the bags of sawdust into the cart of fertilizer and headed outside to check. "Where is that girl?" she inquired under her breath. "Out to lunch?"

Nothing could have prepared her for what she saw when the bell dinged as she stepped back out into the sunshine.

Outside was Lenoir looking uncharacteristically disturbed and unkempt. Her hair which was tucked into a neat looking bun had come unfurled, with long strands of her strawberry blonde locks dancing in the wind. Directly across from her was the infamous Casey King, her boyfriend two of the four years of high school. They were always known as Olympic High's most unlikely couple ever due to his participation in every sport the school offered and Lenoir being Lenoir. No one ever understood but they worked great together. Scarlett remembered many times she would accompany them along with her high school boyfriend Mike Donahue. The double dates usually consisted of going to the food court, hanging out at one of Casey's teammates houses after practice in the Palisades or filming lame videos. Occasionally, Casey's brother would buy them beer, but it was always Mike, Scarlett and Casey drinking it. Lenoir was always lost in one of her fever dreams or making plans to protest something at school. It never stopped her from willing to get silly with them when the moment occurred, but usually she was all business.

Now, here they were, having a heated conversation like an old married couple in the middle of Lyons Street, drawing a crowd. Casey was talking about how long he's been waiting, and she kept repeating hallmark phrases like, "let the past be the past," and "you can still find your path."

"Why do you insist on making me look like an idiot every time I try and talk to you?" Casey pleaded.

Scarlett hadn't caught up with him in a while. He became a bit depressing after high school. He turned down a partial scholarship to play Lacrosse at Marquette University and took a job at a hardware store. "Oh," Scarlett thought aloud as she realized it was the same store. Casey hadn't been doing well in the four years since then. She had gone out with him a few times in Lenoir's absence overseas, but he always had his sights fixed on her. He never stopped talking about her to anyone who would listen. It seemed unhealthy and a bit creepy to Scarlett. That was why she had cut contact with him.

"When are you going to start looking forward? There is a lot of life out there to be lived Casey. We were just a short pit stop."

"When are you ever going to get your head out of the clouds and start living down here?" he countered.

Scarlett wondered if she should intervene. She thought it would make her a good friend to step up against Casey and call him out on his bullshit, but she also didn't want the conversation to end. She reveled in the drama and found it would also fuel her for an afternoon of great conversation and gossip with Lenoir after it was done.

"You have to forget about me," her tone became firmer. "Don't forget about the times we had, no one can take that away from you, but you have to stop thinking about a future possibility of me, Casey."

"Why? Which corner of the world are you fleeing to now? Did you ever think if you were able to face your problems you wouldn't have to run away all the time?"

"What did you think I was doing out there? Biding my time? I was travelling and getting experience and I can't begin to tell you what that can do for your soul and how it can shed light on the questions you never even knew you had. I've got my answers now Casey and I'm better off for it."

"Great, you have all the answers – terrific! Then answer me this, 'Why did you make me wait for you all this time if you are just going to brush me off?'"

Scarlett visibly cringed, but still was enjoying every minute of it.

"Casey, I told you then and I will tell you now, we are over. But it doesn't mean your life has to be! Put your faith in the light and see which way it shines. You'll see." She eyed Scarlett and seemed to remember something. She turned to go, but he caught her by the wrist.

"You can't tell me you still don't have feelings for me. Why did you come back?"

"I live here, duh. Would you let go of me please?" the disturbed face came back to her, causing Scarlett to take a step back. For someone as strong as Lenoir, it made it seem like the whole world was going to end when she made that face.

"Please don't do this to me," he grew more desperate. He let go of her wrist and she stared at him, crossing her arms.

He took off the hardware store smock that consisted of his uniform and put up his hands in a peaceful motion. "Let's just go somewhere and talk. Nothing is coming out right. I have had so much to say to you, and I would really appreciate it if you could hear me out. We can go get coffee. You still drink coffee?"

She shook her head. "We don't have anything left to say. We are two distant clouds headed in opposite directions."

He looked pained for a moment, he tried to take in what she was saying. "Oh, I see. So, you are this 'experienced' world traveler now and I am just some townie, is that it? No more use for dumbfuck Casey?"

"Why are you trying to frame it that way? You know that is not what I am saying."

"Then what are you saying?"

"I'm saying I have reached a peace I can't come back from. This place has touched me, and I have come back to make peace with it before I go back. Every corner of life

[171]

needs peace Casey. I truly hope you can find yours," she turned to leave again and this time he grabbed her arm.

"So, this double talk your speaking, you have a boyfriend, is that it?"

"I have found love. But not like what we had. It is a different kind of love. One that touches you in every way. I don't think you are ready to understand that."

He pulled her closer and his face grew menacing. Scarlett could sense her friend's fear and started over to finally intervene. The scene had turned ugly. He was whispering angrily to her now as she struggled in his grasp but was trying not to make it any worse than it already was.

Scarlett only heard parts of sentences in their frenzied murmurs to one another. She caught his voice saying *meant to be* and hers answering softly back, trying to keep him at bay. This brought back another memory of high school. It was the day Casey and Lenoir broke up in fact. The boy had an anger problem, and even though she said he never touched her, Scarlett saw the faint bruise on the back of her neck the next Saturday they were trying on clothes at Bloomingdales. The thing was, even after scenes like these, Lenoir always spoke well of him. She had every opportunity to trash his name and ruin his reputation, but she never did. She only spoke of his big heart and the person inside he rarely ever showed, which was what must have attracted her to him in the first place.

Something in their conversation took an even uglier turn, because Lenoir began shouting in a voice that didn't seem real. "No, let me go! Let go of me. That's not going to happen!" It all came about so fast because the next thing Scarlett knew, Casey had his hands around her neck. He had an insane look on his face, one mixed with stoicism and nonchalance, yet his eyes were furious and full of fire. Lenoir fought back and what ensued next was unfathomable. Scarlett found herself racing on her heels to jump in the fray, all the while the crowd just watched awestruck. A couple of the men chastised Casey for what he was doing, but their voices came in and out like streams of fog. None of the men backed up the words with actions, so Scarlett felt it was up to her.

Casey saw her approach and seemed to loosen his hands as if she confused him in some way. She was about to scratch the shit out of his arm and face, but instead was t-boned by figures dressed in white. She was knocked to the ground face forward, she put her hands in front of her which took the brunt of the fall, but not without a little road rash. Once the shock of the sting wore off, she turned to see two men in white robes working over Casey. They were wrangling him like a child that was about to cross the street into oncoming traffic. It wasn't a malicious beating, but more of an intervention as if showing Casey that violence couldn't be the right solution to this equation. They were sure of their skills, because once they feel they had incapacitated him, they glanced directly at Lenoir.

Even more shocking was that there was a hint of recognition on her face. She was still visibly upset but did her best to keep her composure as she coughed, gasped and gripped her own throat. The men then turned to Scarlett, one was East Indian, the other of Asian descent. There was a strange sort of contentment in their eyes, a familiar look. However, when they looked upon Scarlett, they looked fearful. They looked back to Lenoir, and she shook her head at them. She did know them!

And with that, they left just as soon as they appeared. Scarlett wanted to track them, but Lenoir's hoarse cough brought her priorities back. She groaned as she got herself up, looking at her translucent, skinned knee that hadn't started to bleed yet. The palms of both of her hands had also been torn up, but not terribly so. Her adrenaline was still pumping, and she worried it would be more painful once it ran out.

Scarlett didn't know if she wanted to hug Lenoir or kick Casey in the groin first, either would have been satisfactory. "Are you okay?" she asked Lenoir.

Still gasping, but no longer bent in half, she nodded. "Do you want me to call someone?" Scarlett realized that her adrenaline *had* run out and the whole scene became something of nightmare rather than the lover's quarrel she had hoped. Her guilt ratcheted up as the realization of what occurred dawned on her.

"I'm fine," Lenoir croaked.

Scarlett turned to the crowd which had begun to dissipate, but still gawked. "Thanks for all the help, dipshits!" she scolded them.

Then she turned her wrath toward Casey. "And you, if I ever see you come near me or my girl again, I'm going to set your pathetic little world on fire." He regarded her but said nothing. He was touching a partially split lip he must have received from the fall. The men in white had vanished, but they had been gentle in their removing him from Lenoir. This made Scarlett nervous because Casey might not be hurt enough to leave them alone.

"This doesn't have anything to do with you," he grimaced getting halfway up and then falling back down again. He stared at Lenoir and wiped more blood off his lip.

She had been recovering but looked okay enough to move now. The rate at which she regained her composure was astonishing to Scarlett. It became more concerning than Casey.

Lenoir moved toward him, locking eyes. "You remember that time in ninth grade? That Friday night after homecoming? We weren't driving yet, and Jody and Norm left without us to go to that party out in Fontana. So, we hopped a couple of bikes and rode in the dark. You remember? We went out to Virginia Avenue Park. It was pitch black and we sat in the kiddie slide for most of the night."

"Noir let's just go-" Scarlett started, but Lenoir held her back.

"I remember we talked for hours. It was the first time you let me kiss you. It was incredible that feeling. Sitting on the slide, trying to find at least one star in the sky," he laughed a nervous laugh and spit blood from his lip. "You said it was the most magical night of your life. You remember that?"

She stared at Casey with penetrating eyes, so much that even *he* looked away. "Casey, I do remember that night. It *was* magical. So magical that I know in my heart of hearts that you are the only mistake I will never forget."

They strolled up the avenue, toward their original destination, Market Place. However, Scarlett was hardly thinking about shopping now. She eyed Lenoir as they walked in silence, the only sound was her heels hitting the pavement with pinpoint precision. Every so often, she would glance back to see if Casey was following, but he was never there. She wounded him. Much more than he had her.

"Don't you think we should talk about it?" she finally broke out of her numb daze as they rounded their third corner.

"You said it best yourself. The boy is hopeless. Besides, the light has taught me to look in and out, but not behind. I can't change the past any more than I can change the future."

"What about all of your supplies at the hardware store?" she asked as an afterthought.

"Oh," Lenoir stopped, but then seemed to remember something. "I'm having them delivered."

Scarlett thought that was strange. The whole day had been turning out nothing like she thought it would. Lenoir went out of her way to go to the hardware store. Did she know Casey worked there? Did she know those men dressed in robes would show up? What else was she not telling her?

"I don't understand," Scarlett held her head, unable to shake all the questions.

"They know my dad real well. It will reach us. Have faith."

"No, I mean the whole Casey thing."

Lenoir stopped and looked her friend deep in the eyes. It was the same look she had given Casey, the one that made him recoil into the warmth of happier times. It made Scarlett feel lonely all over again, having to peel back the layers of Lenoir's defense. She felt like she finally understood what Alice had been saying ever since Lenoir had come back. Then, out of nowhere, Noir said, "I haven't been to 'A new chapter' in forever. She walked around Scarlett as if they hadn't been discussing anything important at all. It felt dismissive. So much so that she remained there on the sidewalk, staring at the spot Lenoir had been until she called after her. "Come on!"

Another bell on another door rang as Lenoir entered the bookstore they frequented so often on those shopping weekends. Scarlett turned to follow and ran straight into a man in a gray overcoat.

"I'm sorry there, young lady." He sounded like he would have tipped a hat in her direction if he wore one. An old-fashioned gentleman that normally she would engage, but instead she eyed him suspiciously, no longer in the mood to converse with randoms.

Joining Lenoir inside, they stalked around the aisles of books, calendars and knick-knack gifts in silence. Scarlett felt those eyes on her as she grazed her fingers over the spines. Lenoir tried to make superficial conversation, "Hmm, I cannot wait until ghanoush is back in season," while they scanned the cookbooks. In the next row over, she spotted a book on face paint, "You remember when you went through that phase where you wanted to be a make-up artist? You were all ready to move out to Century City and join the ranks of the Hollywood keys?"

Scarlett stared at her but said nothing. She could play this game as long as Lenoir could. She would wait her out until she was willing to talk about something real. They continued to look around. The next aisle held sports biographies. After that were music CDs. A momentarily lapse of indulgence unfolded for Scarlett when she spotted the newest single by *Nelly* she had been meaning to pick up, but she quickly chased it back out of her mind.

She could tell it was working with Lenoir. She was giving her the same sad, puppy dog look a guy would when she gave him the silent treatment for ignoring her calls or talking to some girl she didn't like. Scarlett was aware it was manipulative, but she had to find another way. She didn't have the talents her other friends had, so she had to resort to tactics that worked for her. As they meandered aimlessly to another aisles of books, she remembered another game the two of them would play. They would scan the titles on the shelf and pick out items that would reflect on how they were feeling in any given moment. "Feelin' is healing," she remembered aloud.

Lenoir glanced up at her, holding her finger on the book she last looked at, saving her place. At first, she didn't seem to remember at all. She crinkled her nose and looked genuinely confused.

As Scarlett scanned the shelves for an appropriate title, a wry smile formed at the corners of Lenoir's lips. Then it jumped out at her instantly since they had found themselves in the self-help aisle. She grabbed the book, pretending to hide it before the big reveal. She made a show of turning it around the way Vanna White might turn a consonant on the letter board. The title was *Good and Angry: exchanging frustration for character.*

It could have been the sight of the book (which had a strange, disturbed looking woman on the cover), it may have been the goofy face Scarlett made when she revealed the title or perhaps it was the nostalgia factor, but Lenoir snickered loudly. She covered her mouth, as if it were inappropriate to laugh at. Scarlett thought that would be the end of it, but she served it right back by grabbing one that had *Strange Occurrences* written on its spine.

Scarlett nodded in agreement with the message and searched for the next one. It took a bit, but the rule was no one could display two titles in a row. It was a back and forth and Lenoir waited patiently for her partner's selection, trailing her as she buzzed into the theology aisle. Scarlett didn't want to just lob it, she wanted to find something that was perfect. She felt like she had an inside track to Lenoir's mind and might be able to reach her in a way that both Alice and Ramona could not. Then she saw it, she nearly squeaked when it caught her eye. It was perfect. It should not have been as much fun as it was, communicating these feelings in such a juvenile way, but it finally felt like she was gaining back some ground.

She exited the aisle with the book in her arms like a baby and proudly displayed it, *Where is God when it hurts?* The giggles that ensued brought plenty of disconcerting stares and looks of annoyance from the other customers in the store. Scarlett was having a hard time catching her breath, but Lenoir became more reserved after a while. Her smile became a look of determination, the only look she can display when she's on a mission. Scarlett hoped it wasn't moving her away again. She always seemed to move on to something else just when things were getting comfortable.

While Scarlett put her religious book back, she went the long way around to give her friend more time for her next selection. She circled back to the self-help section to see if she could find a title that referenced something about ex-boyfriends. Casey and the whole ugly situation had not completely escaped her mind. Surely, she had seen more shocking things, the time the guy at the club had part of his ear sliced off when his party scuffled with some rougher biker types came to mind. There was also the bad car accident her father had driven them by on the way home from Palm Springs when she was a kid. It was the only time she had seen a dead body, and the image had burned into her young mind.

She wasn't sure why she couldn't just shake this thing with Casey though. Was it because Lenoir was always so put together? Seeing her in the type of situation that should have been more familiar to Scarlett, was that what was troubling her? She hadn't known, but the more she thought about it, the more anxiety it gave her. She kept thinking, *what if I couldn't get him off her? What if those guys hadn't shown up? What if no one would have helped and he would have killed her on a crowdy sunny street in the middle of the day?* What if-

She stopped at the sight of Lenoir shoving her next find into her face. She took it in for a moment. It was a children's book. The cover featured a crudely drawn grassy meadow. In it two little girls from frontier times wore their Sunday dresses with rimmed bonnets to protect their fair skin from the sun. One girl held out a handful of freshly picked posies to the other one, it featured the title spread across it in perfect cursive *I'm sorry Almira Ann* it read.

Scarlett had no idea who Almira Ann was or what had been done to her to warrant the apology, she just knew it was the last straw. The day had been too much. It could have been the title, the meaning behind it or the pained, yet stable look Lenoir wore on her face as she held it up, but suddenly Scarlett burst into tears.

Instantly her face popped capillaries as she reached into her purse for something to hide her shame. Crying was something Scarlett didn't do, not in public, not anywhere. The fact she couldn't control this emotional outburst was even more embarrassing and disarming. She didn't even want the apology anymore, she just wanted to feel safe somewhere with her friend. She wanted to feel what they had only a few minutes prior. Now it was she who was ruining it. Now it was she who set back the conversation she wanted to have but didn't know how.

So much for feelin' his healing.

There in the middle of the self-help section, Lenoir dropped the book and wrapped her arms around her friend. It felt genuine; perhaps the most genuine gesture Lenoir had taken since she had come back. Scarlett bore her face into Lenoir's bony shoulder to muffle embarrassing sobs.

Lenoir soothingly shushed her as she stroked her hair softly. After what seemed like an eternity, she finally broke the silent pact they held and whispered, "Do you want to get out of here?"

Scarlett nodded as she held her. She did not want to pull her away and face the other people in *The Next Chapter* but had to brave it in order to have the conversation she now knew they needed to have. She took one last fleeting glance at the children's book cover, nearly losing it again at the sight of the two frontier girls and their simple act of forgiveness. Nothing so trite had ever touched her so much.

She had calmed down once they steeled themselves away at Shoop's, a local café and grocer that seemed right out of Southern Italy. Scarlett stirred her peppermint tea absent-mindedly while Lenoir looked her over and waited. Once she felt as if she had a normal rhythm going again, and with the warm tea soothing her unease, it felt like this was her best opportunity.

"What really happened with you guys at the end of school?" Scarlett asked. "I only heard that it happened at the Brentwood party I didn't go to. Of course, I was going to ask you about it afterwards, but that was when you disappeared. Ramona said it was not even evident that you did break up. The only thing that was evident was that you skipped town. I had never been so shocked. I know you had talked about it all the time. How you couldn't wait to get out of here, but I thought you were going to be planning a little more, I didn't think you would just up and leave like that. I think it shocked a lot of us. Including Casey. I know he has it bad for you, and whatever. But until today, I never thought he deserved that."

Lenoir smiled politely. She was considered something a while before she answered. "It probably wasn't evident. You've probably noticed, but nothing I ever intend to do is to directly hurt anyone. Everybody else was making plans. Alice and Ramona were going to school, you got your job. I was making plans along with the rest of you."

"You ever think to share those plans?" Scarlett bugged her eyes out. They felt dry from the tears she had shed.

"Only about a hundred times," Lenoir looked uneasy sharing this.

"Then why?"

"I was worried someone would stop me from going. I didn't want any discouragement and I knew if I didn't go then I might never go. I didn't want to get stuck."

"Stuck? No one was ever going to hold you back Noir. In fact, I have to call bullshit on that entire excuse, because no one has ever been able to talk you out of anything as far as I can tell. Are you saying you didn't want to get stuck with Casey? Or you didn't want to get stuck here?"

"I didn't want to get stuck without a plan, so I made one. And in regard to Casey, we were never a good match. Oh, I loved him, no one can ever deny that, but I am not the same person I was back then."

Scarlett eyed her peppermint tea, but declined another sip, the sour feeling returning to her stomach. "Is he the same person? Was that the real Casey we saw today? Has he hurt you before?"

Lenoir stared off. She closed her eyes, concentrating on something. Scarlett wasn't sure she had heard her and was about to repeat the question.

"Casey is no longer the same person either, but he's stuck without a plan. You see the difference? That wasn't going to happen to me. I couldn't let it."

"I know you guys never really seemed to be much of a match," Scarlett admitted. "You never made sense as a couple. Look, I get it. If you were just wanting to get acquainted with guys, I totally get it. I understand that more than being deeply and madly in love. I always assumed I'd know it when I'd see it. After a while, it just started being pushed from my mind more and more until one day I never thought about it at all. You realize that's because it doesn't exist, right?"

"True love *does* exist," Lenoir corrected her. "You just have to look in the right place."

"Where is the right place?"

Lenoir looked around, pausing before sharing an observation, "I don't think it could be found in this place. It's too dark."

"Now look here, you can ream Casey, school, our lives after high school all you want, but you leave home out of it. This is the most exciting city in the world! Where else can you find Hollywood, the best shopping, the beach, endless sunny days and the hottest looking people in the world all in the same place?" she sounded more defensive than she meant to, but she meant every word. "I don't care how superficial that sounds."

"Isik once told me, 'Superficiality is gazing at one thing obsessively, where love is all things looking outward in the same direction.' That's what it feels like, finding your place in the world. It is not just you by yourself. If I had set off to go on an adventure, I would have been back a lot sooner and a lot more in debt. But what I found was my place. *The* place actually. It wasn't me by myself. It was

[182]

me and a collective of everything. Being all in one can feel powerful. But what happened next made me feel like God. What I am given will make me feel immortal."

Scarlett shook her head, "I don't think I will ever feel that way about anyone. I don't think I am capable of it. I don't think I would ever let myself get to that point. I never felt superficial. Guys are superficial. They don't care how you are feeling, they don't care what their actions do to you, all they care about is their credibility."

"You don't think they feel the same as you do."

"Doubt it. They are too busy feeling which way their boner is swinging to think about much else."

"You must realize that not every guy is like that."

"I don't think every guy is like that," Scarlett said defensively. "I think everyone and everything is like that. Of course everyone is in it for themselves."

"You don't really believe that."

"Weren't you paying attention today? What was everyone else doing on the street when Casey had his hands around your throat? What was I doing? I was selfishly waiting for drama to happen so that I could witness it," Scarlett confessed.

"People get scared, it doesn't mean they're selfish. Those people were afraid."

"Of Casey? Please, the boy has gotten soft," Scarlett scoffed. "I'm getting good at recognizing bullshit when I see it, Noir. I've heard quite a lot in my day."

"Those people were not afraid of Casey; they were afraid to reach out. Afraid to put themselves out there. They were afraid of what would happen if they made a connection. This is how much of the world operates Scarlett. It is not unique to just us. The dark teaches us to miss what is right in front of us."

"How about another example?" Scarlett felt discombobulated, she knew Lenoir did not mean it personally, but that was how she took it.

[183]

"Okay."

"Here's one that happened to me a couple of years ago. Of course, you know things changed for all of us after high school, whether we went globe-trotting or not. They changed for me drastically. I found myself in a whole new circle since you were gone, and our other girls went to school upstate. I made friends with my co-workers, first at the boutique than the club. The club kids just worked there for the discount and to be seen every night. For them it was all about image. Image is hard to keep up with if you don't have a trust fund, believe me.

"I had a chance this one time to date a guy who would hardly give the b-list actresses the time of day. I'm not sure what he did, but it had something to do with finance, so he knew everyone in this town. He handled the very thing that kept the dreams going, so he was of an important status. Of all the people that night for some reason, he was interested in me. It was what the audition whores call your big break, right? I wasn't even into him that much, but I knew it would be a big break all the same.

"The guy asks if I want to go out and I stupidly start writing my phone number down on his cocktail napkin. They all laugh like I am a little kid who just did something adorable, and I am one step away from ditching out of there. Then he comes up real close to me and whispers *I mean do you want to go out right now?* I didn't understand and everyone else seemed to be in on the joke but me. I didn't want to be the clueless girl standing there, asking everyone what he meant by it. I just went with the flow even though I didn't know where it was going. So, I say *But we are already out.* This gets an even bigger laugh and I laughed along with them even though I was completely freaking out inside.

"He takes me by the hand and that was when the laughing stopped. They all looked at me like I was royalty. I certainly felt like a princess the way he led me away. I got a couple of fist pumps from some of the girls I knew, and I felt like a hero or something. Like I just had saved a busload of kids from a burning wreck. It was like floating, the music, the wind from the speakers, the lights moving above me. Even as we made our way through the dancefloor it felt like the sea of people were parting just in awe of us.

"Well, I wasn't paying enough attention, because before I realized it, I was in the men's bathroom. There were a couple of dudes in there leering. I could hear them putting their big fat stupid heads up to the stall he took me into. It was gross and seedy and disgusting; I didn't know how something so beautiful could turn so ugly so quickly. There's puke on the floor and shit running halfway down the bowl. When I looked back to him, his hair looked greasy and in the light his face looked the same. I realized he was wearing make-up and it made him look old and used up. I know I would have to in order to keep my status, but he wouldn't put one on. I begged him, I was hitting him in the back, but I couldn't get enough leverage because the stall was so small.

"I remember screaming at the top of my lungs. I remember the dude's arms outside of the stall reaching under and grabbing my legs. I lost a shoe and my brand-new stockings dragged through the piss, toilet water and whatever else was on the floor. I never felt so shitty in all my life," she paused to wipe her face with her napkin. The spot where the tears returned burned from the dryness of the old ones. She felt a chunk of mascara formulate underneath as she wiped it away.

"When it was over, he just strolled out casually. I was so upset I thought I was going to explode, but I had to keep my composure because I was still worried about my status amongst the others. I know it makes no sense, I know I should have been in fight or flight mode, but I was weirded out that it bothered me so much. I just kept telling myself over and over *It's just sex, it's just bathroom scum, nothing that can't be washed off or forgotten.* Compared to what I thought was coming my way, I thought it was easily worth it, even though it was probably the most disgusting thing I had ever done. I didn't leave the bathroom until another one of the guys tried to get into the stall with me, yelling *Train* to the other morons.

"I took a deep breath and joined the others. Well, they saw it all over my face because right away they were asking me what was wrong and why I looked ill. The finance guy kept telling them, *I think she had too much to drink. Should I call her a taxi? I think she's drunk, maybe we should find someone to take her home.* I talked to one girl, Samantha, in private. She was from Reseda, and I thought maybe she would understand where I was coming from since she wasn't born into money like the others were. *He was bad, wasn't he?* She kept trying to guess what it was. *Bad breath? Minute man? It must have had something to do with the sex.* I only shook my head, over and over again. He wouldn't wear a condom, I told her. She looked at me like I just told her my hair was on fire even though it obviously wasn't. *Just take the morning after* she said like I was whining like a little kid. She was going to leave, and I yelled that he raped me. *Your drunk,* she told me, *you're not making sense. Go home, and for your own sake do not tell anyone else that.* So, are you going to tell me Lenoir that she was just afraid of the consequences of backing me up? That she was so scared for me that she responded to my cry for help so irrationally? Because if you are, save it. She was just angling for a way to use it to raise her own status. I know she was telling them all when I left from the way they looked at me. You think they were all just afraid? No, they didn't care. People are only in it for themselves." She repeated, feeling slightly better about this burden she carried around with her so long that she had forgotten how heavy it really was.

Lenoir had that considerate look again. It was nothing resembling her previous warmth, it was almost superficial in itself as if demonstrating what Scarlett had just laid out. More polite responses came out of her, but her song was the same. She was so damn stubborn, Scarlett wondered if it was already too late. "I think there are many people in this world who will help if you let them in. Those people were scared and anyone who is scared deserves our help if they let us in. Only when they help themselves can they help others. The point is everyone needs help sometimes."

"Really, I find that hard to believe. Have you ever needed help? After you left, I mean?"

Lenoir looked surprised, "Of course! When you are searching is when you need the most help, and I found many warm nights from the kindness of others. I will never be able to repay them for what they did for me, but I can try."

"And what is that going to do for you?"

"It will bring me more and more into the light. You'll see. People surprise you. I continue to be surprised by what people will or will not do. Do not feel down on them. You may be too afraid to give them enough of a chance."

"You think what happened to me was me not 'giving them enough of CHANCE?!' Scarlett never felt as angry about the whole situation as she had right there.

"Of course not, all I mean is that you can't give up on people and finding their inner light."

"Shut up about the light Lenoir! We are sick and tired of hearing about it. We want to hear from you! Not your cult! I ask again, when have you ever needed help with anything?"

"I needed your help today at the hardware store and you gave it."

"Uh-huh, and let me guess, you were helping Casey find himself finally after going to that store of all stores. Be straight with me, I know you are not telling me something."

"Only the darkness hides secrets."

She rolled her eyes, "Then tell me something you need help with, and I will be there. Anything Lenoir, please name it."

"You saw them, right?"

"What?"

"My help. They were never going to let Casey hurt me or you," she assured.

Scarlett stared at her in disbelief. She shook her head. What she knew of Lenoir was sitting in front of her, but she was no longer Noir at all. Everyone had been right about her all along.

Upset, the dismay could no longer be contained on Scarlett's face. She stood up abruptly, not even digging money out of her purse for her peppermint tea and left without word.

Proving her point even more, Lenoir remained behind without so much of a call after her. She sat there staring off, seeming like a small part of her was preventing the rest from taking it all back.

Scarlett streamed through people out on the sidewalk with stinging, misty eyes. The marketplace was in full Saturday afternoon swing now. The tables were set up, the merchants were out and spring promised to be around sooner than originally thought. Scarlett stomped through them, hurting more than she had in a long time. She ran headlong into a man passing out flyers and summoning petitions in front of the ice cream parlor a few doors down from the café.

He glowered at first, but then went right into his spiel about how badly the mental health crisis is getting. "We are gathering petitions today to tell the governor that mental illness is a health crisis, not a stigma. Look at what the rhetoric is doing to people in this country," he explained. "Look at that poor boy from upstate. You think his taste for American culture just stopped and completely turned inside out the moment he landed on foreign soil. No, his mental disorder went undiagnosed for years and only when it affected us, the spoiled youngest child of all nations, do we cry foul. But instead of helping him, we do not-" he paused as one of his fellow petitioners was repeating the same speech nearly verbatim a moment after him, giving him an echo he was trying to shake. "No- we are going to lock him up and throw away the key! So how about it, eh?" he pushed the clipboard towards Scarlett.

Later, after more crying on a park bench and more pretzels from her favorite stand than she cared to count, she was on her cell listening to the other end ringing. To her dismay, she was greeted with the voicemail greeting, "Hey, you've reached Ramona, you know what to do." BEEP

She repeated the steps, this time phoning Alice up at school. She had no idea what she was going to say to them, she just wanted to let them know they were not alone. She had not abandoned them. She wanted to desperately reach out and this was the only way she knew how.

"Hello?" an unfamiliar voice answered.

"Alice?"

"Alice isn't here right now. Do you want me to give her a message?"

"No message," she let Alice's roommate disconnect the call. She held the plastic phone up to her ear for the longest time; after it became too heavy she let gravity take it. She thought maybe she'd drown in another round of tears, but instead she threw her phone out into the park by which she sat and let a guttural yell of frustration go. It turned a few heads – her tantrum – but far fewer than anyone but Scarlett would have expected. "Figures," she watched the faces doing their best to ignore her. She thought about what the man had said on the sidewalk earlier, that it isn't a stigma.

He was wrong.

Anything that isn't happy, joyful, normal, habitual, a custom, a trend or expected is a stigma.

"Excuse me, dear?" an older woman approached her as she was about to leave. "Do you need help?"

Scarlett looked her in the eye. She did not have the heart to lie anymore. "There's no such thing."

Part 8

You Can't Go Home Again

So, where are you?

Now that the time is upon us, where is your spirit? Where is your mind in all of this? You've wavered and struggled, but now you're rooted. Our plans are solidified, and our spirits and mind embolden you for your assignment. We gave you your purpose, we ignited your passion and now you can channel it to achieve something greater than yourself.

Your struggles are not easy, none ever are, but Isik is proud of you!

He loves you. We all do.

We are all in awe of you and will be long after your light fades. This is the single most selfless act anyone has ever done for us, and no gift this great has ever been given to the world. You will bring the light to the masses, for the darkness has ruled for too long.

Isik spoke of you last night, once the light has reached them, he will join you in paradise. You and he will live together in Jannah. In Daw aba-de-le-a (Eternal light).

He speaks about when you first came to him: raw, full of passion, but no outlet to contain your outrage, your sense of injustice. He knows you care so deeply about this garden and its inhabitants. He sensed your burning desire to make a change from the moment you came to him.

How fair you were, you and your novice spirit. Together with us, you've witnessed the start of a new era. One that will lead the populous to your light. We know you can bring it to them. You used to be them. Your burden has been established. Your companions are ready for you. You just call them by their name, and they will come for you. The church of dissenters will be out of session soon.

You will bring them to a new faith, one which they will flock toward once you show them they can fly. Tolerance of their ways has been tried. Can you accept this injustice for what it is after all the harm it has caused you being there? You couldn't when you first reached out – that is why our union is destiny.

This will be our last communication with you. Go forth brave, young angel. Avenge us from ourselves. Isik implores you. Remember his words and his teachings as you are brought into the full breadth of the light. Remember his words and his wisdom. Embrace it, channel it to make the world a new and better place.

Into the fire we will throw you, and from the fire you will return to us.

Until we reach the next plane, that is all any of us can do. Goodbyes are only difficult if the next realm is unknown.

Harmony and affection always.

Last resorts make beautiful new beginnings.

So, before the world falls on itself and is brought to its fate, remember not the man, but his teachings. Like the others have told you, you can cry, you can yearn, you can get lost, you will get burned. You can wish the world well and do it in vain, but what you cannot do is go home again.

"You mean you've really never been on one?" Piper asked her sister skeptically.

"I saw a Pakistani fellow looking through what looked like a stock portfolio in a café near Fazilka, but I couldn't make much sense of it," Lenoir shook her head.

"Yeah, but you remember going online when you were in school?"

"I think I had an email address in 12th grade, but I never really used it. So, tell me, sister. What do you use it for?"

Piper's gaze slowly fell upon her. It had been a strange week. Lenoir had pretty much moved into her room. Piper, fine with the company and attention for once at first relished it but became more uncomfortable as time went on. She knew Dad and Lenoir were not getting along. Anyone within a mile radius of the house could feel that. She thought at first that Lenoir was hiding herself away from him, but she never seemed to go completely out of her way to ignore him either.

She would mostly read from her weird book written partly in English and she would make phone calls and spoke gibberish with randoms late at night. One time Piper found her kneeling on the floor and striking some kind of yoga pose and worshipping the wall. She thought maybe her big sister was cracking up. She also thought she had changed quite a bit from what she remembered. "You want to see my website?"

"You can have your own website?" Lenoir asked excitedly.

"Yeah duh, anyone can," Piper savored a rare moment when she knew something Lenoir did not.

She showed her. She showed her the drawings she had made, the comments on her message board. She even let her read some of her poetry, which she had never shown anyone before. There was another thing she had forgotten in the time Lenoir had been away. One thing Piper had learned from an early age, that no matter who you were, when Lenoir paid attention to you, it felt like you were the only person in the world. She had not lost any of that charisma, and most people were helpless to fall under her spell.

"What's a Geocity? I like the sound of that. Not your city, not my city, but our city," Lenoir said excitedly.

"It's just the name of the website." In addition to her smugness, Piper also felt empowered to show her world-traveled sister something she didn't already know.

"So, I notice you use a lot of dark colors, I like the shades of purple in that tall guy's fedora. They really stand out amongst the gray. It looks like you've captured his forlorn mood."

Piper nodded, "Yeah, I call him Mr. Unremembered. He's doomed to travel the earth until someone can recognize him, but he's been at it for so long there is no one left to remember him. Most people don't see what is right in front of them. He tries out different colors in order to be noticed, but so far it hasn't worked for him. He seems to agree with purple most of the time," her confidence started to waver.

Lenoir placed a hand on her shoulder, "I think there is no better representation of the loneliness that people can feel. The world can be a very lonely place, no matter who you are or where you come from."

"A couple people online have said he's too depressing, but screw them, I was thinking about making it into a comic. Maybe even making it a full book."

Lenoir gently took her sister's face and held it, "I think you are going to do great things Piper."

She shrugged out of her hold, "Yeah whatever, Dad doesn't think so."

"Why would you think that?"

"He barely looks at me," she hated how it sounded, but there was no sugarcoating the truth. Her confidence finally snapped, and her reaction made her feel like Mr. Unremembered, a harsh reminder of the loneliness.

"He's just going through some stuff right now," regret clouded Lenoir's face.

"Yeah, what did you do to him?"

"I think he thinks I'm not on the right path, but I'm trying to assure him, and you too, I am right where I need to be. Everyone gets lonely sometimes. I think even with the three of us together again, we are all feeling it in a way. I think I upset the balance a bit by coming back. I want you to know that I want to restore what may have been missing and allow this household to heal. I don't think I've done that yet. I think it would be better if I was left out of the equation."

"Is that why you're leaving again?"

Lenoir nodded, "Part of the reason. Another part is that I have a calling I have to answer."

Piper laughed, "I've never heard anyone call college 'a calling' before."

"We all have callings or however you want to refer to them. If we don't answer them, then how can we answer to ourselves?"
Piper changed the subject before Lenoir went off on one of her earthy, new age tangents, "What time will your friends be here?"

Her sister brought out that tractor beam of a smile again, the first hint of the person she used to be that Piper had seen in weeks, "Soon."

Once Lenoir had left to greet her guests, Piper was alone again. She started crafting a new sketch of Mr. Unremembered; she was halfway through his face when her friend Benny chimed in on her messenger:

TWENTYTIMES_BENNY03: You think we are in the clear?

[196]

Piper rolled her eyes, Benny was her best friend, but the way he stressed over the small details was ironic considering how much of a rebel he considered himself to be.

PIPERTHESNIPER: Yeah, duh, we didn't get caught did we?

TWENTYTIMES_BENNY03: Yeah but Teresa is known to talk. The whole school will probably know by Monday, and the teachers after that. You know how word gets around.

PIPERTHESNIPER: Who cares were going to be out of that hellhole and in a deeper ring of hell next year. You think they want to keep us back – for a little egg and TP?

TWENTYTIMES_BENNY03: Yeah, high school's gonna suck!

PIPERTHESNIPER: Ya it will.

TWENTYTIMES_BENNY03: Cool, I just wanted to check and make sure you were keeping cool and not confessing.

PIPERTHESNIPER: Yeah whatever, whos gonna listen anyway?

TWENTYTIMES_BENNY03: Haha, true that! All right, my mom is after me about some shite, later loser.

PIPERTHESNIPER: Later...

The sound of the chime of Benny leaving the chat echoed in Piper's head. It gave her a headache. There was laughter and a clamor of dishes as people laughed downstairs. She really didn't want to make an appearance at this party, maybe she would wait a little longer until some of the relatives left. They were always asking her the same dumb questions and it bugged the hell out of her.

She meditated on Benny a bit more. Something in their conversation brought her mind back to Lenoir. She would tell someone if she thought it would do any good, but it was too crazy, and no one would believe her anyway. It bugged her so much she clicked off her work-in-progress sketch of Mr. Unremembered and played some Eminem to drown out the din from downstairs.

There was another time she could have said something and didn't, again reasoning that no one would listen. Something about it felt like a missed opportunity. That maybe things could have been different if she had spoken up.

When she was ten, she remembered being in that Kenan & Kel phase real bad and watching a lot of Nicksplat with her friends on sleepovers. She cringed thinking how lame she had been. She didn't hang out with any of those girls anymore. They had all joined debate teams and started wearing makeup and carving names of boys they liked into their arms and legs. She had told herself many times over the years that she outgrew them, and it always made her feel marginally better.

She remembered waking up during that phase to some clatter. It was June gloom, hot and gray. Another party had occurred earlier that evening. It was Lenoir's grad party. She had a ton of friends of course, and they all stopped by to ask what she was going to do now, to which she had kept repeating the same refrain back, "I have my plans." Even her dorky boyfriend had come. She heard through the grapevine that he ditched his own grad party so he could come to hers. He was always following her around like some kind of pathetic lost puppy, and she led him around more or less on a leash.

She, what's-his-name and her friends had gone out later that night. Piper had gone to her room and was reading. She had read over 20 books that summer, she thought she was reading *Holes* at the time, but couldn't be sure. She had fallen asleep with the light on again, but when she woke up to that noise, it was out. It was Lenoir that had woken her. At the time, she figured she had just gotten back, but she was actually leaving.

Since Piper had woken, she took the opportunity to pee. When she came back out, she could see in the dim shadows of the upstairs hall that Lenoir struggled with something. She swayed around in the dark lifting something heavy, knocking it into their mom's old table of vases, sending them whirling but not to the point of falling over.

She remembered asking, still in a daze from being half asleep, "What are you doing?"

Startled, Lenoir's face shot up out of the darkness, "Nothing, just moving some of this old stuff out of my room."

"Now? In a suitcase?" Piper could make out the object once her eyes had adjusted to the dark.

"Yeah," Lenoir laughed awkwardly, "Dumb I know, but I just had a bug and you know how I get when I'm on a mission. Go back to bed Pipe, I'm just bringing it out to the garage, so I don't have to look at it anymore."

"Lenoir, what's going on?" she rubbed her sleepy face but could still tell something wasn't right.

Lenoir sighed in the dark of the hallway, her shadow slumping slightly. It was a long time before she answered, so long in fact, Piper had wondered if she had fallen asleep standing up. Just as she was about to give up, Lenoir found her voice again, "I broke up with Casey tonight. This is all the stuff that reminds me of him, and I don't want to think about it right now. I want to get out! I mean, I just want it all out of my room."

Piper nodded, sleepiness winning her over from any real concern. At the time it seemed only partial odd, Lenoir was always doing odd things, and this was no different. But even with how tired she was, something ate at her enough to ask, "You're coming back though, right?"

"I will return, I promise," Lenoir hurried past her with the suitcase, no longer struggling. "Love you sis," was the last thing she heard her whisper as she descended the stairs, the suitcase thumping down on each step. There was no way dad would have heard her because he had terrible insomnia in those days and would take three Ambien a night just to get to sleep. In hindsight, Piper wished she would have screamed at the top of her lungs. By the next evening when she had returned to bed, Lenoir was long gone. She left a note, but it brought her and her dad no solace.

She had abandoned them.

She took off in the middle of the night like she was escaping from prison. She wouldn't see her sister again for four years, which to Piper seemed like an eternity. She had her dead to rights right there in the hallway and she just let her go. She often thought back to that situation as the only thing she ever regretted in her life. The rest she could take or leave but letting her sister slip through her fingers like that.

Yeah – things could have been a lot different had she spoken up. Things were never really the same after that. In fact, they still weren't.

She was jolted out of this waking remembrance like Lenoir making the racquet with the suitcase in the hallway had woke her all over again. It was her aunt Clara's voice this time, her late mother's much older sister, beckoning her downstairs to 'make an appearance' as she put it. Piper didn't want to go, but suddenly the room she shared with the stranger that was her sister seemed to grow cold. She shivered her way out the door and reluctantly descended the same set of stairs Lenoir dragged her suitcase down all those years ago.

She tried to put on a fake smile for the remaining relatives as she descended, but the chill of that memory seemed to chase after her.

"There she is, so kind of you to join us," Aunt Clara exaggerated.

While she was only one of two aunts Piper had, she actually had no deep affection or hatred for the woman. Even though Clara always made comments about Piper's lack of sunshine, her dark clothing and that she didn't eat enough. Piper attributed her lack of attitude for her aunt to the fact that she was her mother's full sister, not to mention a spitting image of the woman.

Even Piper's dad said it was hard to see Clara after mom died due to the resemblance. He said it gave him an uneasy feeling like he was staring at a ghost. Piper remembered questioning her father on whether mom was really a "ghost" or not and being upset by the lack of response. "Here I am," she feigned enthusiasm.

"Oh, it's so lovely to see you girls together again. Let me look at you side by side, I want to snap a photo," Clara shoved Lenoir and Piper together with surprising strength. Piper looked to her dad for moral support, but of course, he was off sulking somewhere not paying the least bit of attention.

"That's a really nice camera, Auntie," Lenoir mentioned as she wrapped her arm around her sister. "You could sell it and feed a whole village," Piper heard her mutter under her breath, which caused her a genuine smile at that sardonic tone.

Clara's fingers worked over the buttons and settings on the camera most ungracefully. When she was satisfied, she inexplicably brought up her thumb and mashed on the shutter. She turned her back and the Adams sisters separated from one another. "Don't go anywhere!" Clara wagged a finger, "I want one with my girls as well – to show your Uncle Al. He was sorry he couldn't be here, but you know how his job is. Excuse me, young lady," she grazed the elbow of Lenoir's friend Alice who was walking by with a tray of snacks from the kitchen. "Would you kindly take a photo of us?" she pushed the camera towards Alice before she could set her plate down.

"Of course I will," Alice placated her.

"You are too kind," Clara heaved herself between them to pose for the photo.

After the photo op, Lenoir seemed to sense Piper's anxiety rising. She grabbed her sister by the arm and pulled her into the den where her friends hung out, firmly separated from the relatives and other acquaintances of the family. "We'll be safe here," Lenoir whispered.

Piper sat in the corner of the couch, seated between Lenoir and some guy wearing a white robe that made him look like he was a mental patient. Lenoir talked with her friends, but Piper's attention was pulled in a million different directions. First, she noticed the glorious food spread across the kitchen table which made her wonder where her father's latest research project had gone. For the past several weeks it seemed like he was always seated at the table, hunched over a million loose leaf papers but not really looking like he was interested in any of it. In their place were trays of crackers, shrimp, meats of all kinds, as well as fruit and veggies on another tray. Some kind of weird cheese fermented in another dish beside that with more things to dip into it. Piper's stomach growled at the sight of it, but she was pinned too far into the couch when Lenoir shoved her over more after another one of her mental patient friends joined them. *Seriously, what is with the robes?*

It was a bit awkward in the den because her new friends seemed to make her high school friends nervous or anxious somehow. Her best girlfriends, Alice and them, all eyed those in the robes suspiciously, looking painfully at Lenoir, them, and back again. It reminded Piper of dad once more, "Lenoir where is dad? Is he not here?"

"He's around here somewhere. I saw him talking to June and Uncle Rob earlier," she turned her attention back towards her friend Ramona. They were talking about college. "I think I'm really going to love Stanford," Lenoir beamed. "I'm so glad they are able to accept me this late in the semester."

"Yeah, how exactly did you swing that?" Ramona asked, side-eyeing Lenoir's couch companions.

"I guess a sizeable donation helps," Lenoir smiled.

"Where you getting your bankroll from?" her friend Scarlett chimed in, "And does he have room for one more?"

Ramona snickered, loosening up a little bit. "Is that what this is? The robes, the healthy glow in their cheeks? You guys are in a sex cult, aren't you?"

Piper laughed out loud, only trying to imagine Lenoir in the sex trade. She couldn't really see her sister prostituting herself out. She could see her running the brothel, but not actively participating beyond that.

Lenoir smiled, and looked to her new friends who Piper found odder by the moment since she never made any introductions, and they never seemed to speak.

"They don't understand a word we are saying, do they?" Ramona laughed, picking up a solo cup and swigging from it.

"They certainly are quiet fellows," Aunt Clara had spotted them again and moved in. "I haven't been able to get them to say anything all night. Very polite nonetheless."

"They're philosophy students," Lenoir explained. "They've taken a vow of silence for a year. They've shed all possessions and labels, including their names."

"Then what do you call them?" Alice, still with the untouched full plate of snacks in her lap asked.

"I call them my apostles."

This stopped Aunt Clara, as well as others within earshot to all stop what they were doing and stare at Lenoir. Unwavering, she brought out that smile again, "I'm totally kidding! They've heard how wonderful the education system is here, they are soon going to be my roomies at Stanford where they will study philosophy."

"At least it will be quiet," Ramona quipped, causing Scarlett to snort next to her.

"Oh, you young people, I could never have imagined living with men when I was your age, but it's a different world now, isn't it Vincent?"

Vincent Adams entered the room, looking just as haggard has he had in past weeks. "What's this?" he asked, also glancing warily at Lenoir's robed entourage. Piper began to regret calling them mental patients at the outset, even if it was just in her head. She was beginning to feel sorry for them, all this negative attention and speculation on them. She wondered even if they couldn't speak English if a small part of them knew they were being openly mocked.

"You're fine with this new living arrangement?" Aunt Clara questioned him, seeming more concerned.

"If it makes you feel better, they also took a vow of celibacy," Lenoir added still seated between them all.

Clara rolled her eyes, "As admirable as that sounds, I must inform you dear niece that I was not born yesterday."

A knock at the door interrupted them.

Just when it was starting to get good, Piper thought.

She tried to lean forward to catch a glimpse of the latest visitor, as her dad hurried to answer it, but Aunt Clara stood in the way. She held a hand on her hip and stared at Lenoir, "So are there any other girls in this club of yours?"

Lenoir smiled, glanced at the fellow next to her, an understanding seemed to emerge between them, "We have very strong women. Women ready to make changes. Women who made the biggest sacrifices but will come through shining brightly on the other side. We need them, just as they need us."

Piper's attention was caught between Clara muttering at that response, dismissing it as psychobabble, and her father addressing the visitor at the door. Her father won out when Clara moved in to ensnare Uncle Rob in a trap of her own brand of psychobabble.

When Vincent moved into the doorway, an old man with sleepy eyes in an old looking suit followed behind him. They were speaking in hushed tones, and the look on Vincent's face almost said he knew this man. *But that's impossible*, Piper's mind reasoned, *dad doesn't have any friends, just co-workers.*

"If I ask her to come over and dismiss all this ridiculous shit you are feeding me, will you please leave my property and never come back?" Vincent's face was worn, haggard – over the past few weeks he seemed to transform into a man as old as the one he stood by. Piper was not sure who she pitied more, her father or herself, because this man made her nervous. Her father's admission made her nervous. *I knew it, Benny snitched to save his own ass. I'm going to punch that kid in the face the next time I see him.*

"If she admits it outright, we may have a problem, Mr. Adams."

"Well don't expect me to help you out when you get dizzy from her talking circles around you," he folded his arms.

"I can handle a teenager. Like I told you before, I have daughters of my own."

Piper stood up. She knew she was about to get busted, so every inclination inside told her to run.

"What is it?" Lenoir's friend, Ramona asked. She looked at Piper worriedly, almost as if she could see the guilt burning her insides.

The knot in Piper's stomach grew three more sizes as she shook her head in reply.

"I don't know what you expect to happen here," Vincent sounded tired, "You can't lock my daughter up for saying dreamy things."

Piper turned toward the kitchen, ready to bolt out the side door they never used if need be. She was already running through her list of friends in her head, a place to hide out until this unwelcome visitor left and everything blew over.

Her father's voice rose behind her, "Wait, Lenoir! This man would like to talk to you."

She turned again, wondering how their own father could confuse them, but Lenoir was up and trailing her. "It's not for you," she assured her.

"What? How did you-?" Piper felt like her head was spinning.

"Don't worry, Pipe, your big sister knows how to handle this."

She stood there, standing awkwardly, confused as what was happening and why. "He doesn't know?"

"Know what?" the man in the black suit asked. "What don't I know?"

Lenoir looked at him, not unkindly. "You are here to speak to me, correct?"

"I am indeed. I've been meaning to speak to you for some time," he took his hat off and extended a hand out to her, which she accepted.

"I sense no light in you," she stated matter-of-factly.

"You know, I'd love to hear more about this 'light.' I've been waiting to hear more about it for some time as well."

"Answers are close at hand, but probably not the ones you're looking for," she assembled and led him into the kitchen. She seemed so fully sure of herself that Piper became embarrassed at her own reaction to his presence. People were curious about what was happening, but at the same time, no one seemed to notice her. Just another example, yet one she welcomed this time, of her being ignored by a room full of people.

They were in there for some time. Lenoir closed the pocket door that connected the living room with the kitchen to give them some privacy.

"Dad? Who is that?"

"It's Oz Nolan, from the agency," he muttered, his voice retreating back to his usual whisper quiet.

"What does he want with Lenoir?"

"Just to talk – I think."

"About what?" she persisted.

"Christ Piper! Give me a break, would you? I don't know. He didn't have any papers, so that's good news, right? It means he just wants to talk. There's nothing he can do. There is no proof of anything out there. Believe me! I checked!"

Lenoir's friends watched him sadly. Everyone seemed to be aware of something Piper was not. Even Aunt Clara. The only people who seemed to have no interest in what was happening behind the kitchen door were the mental patients in the white robes. They brought out these leather-bound books and began to read silently aside one another. They seemed to also be breathing and meditating, but it could have just as well been the tension that eclipsed the room.

After what seemed like an eternity of electric silence, the relatives and adult friends in the next room continued chattering. They were likely bored of waiting, while Lenoir's high school friends and immediate family were on pins and needles. Then Lenoir and Oz emerged from the kitchen. His face had changed dramatically; it was red, flustered and full of anger. He stomped toward the front door, parting the group of people watching everything unfold.

Lenoir followed behind him, "I'll show you out then," her usual air of plastic pleasantness doing its job.

"I was really hoping you wouldn't have to force my hand like this, Ms. Adams. I was told you were of superior intelligence."

"You were also told my answers might not be the ones you were looking for. Do not wait too long on me, sir. My purpose is all but complete."

He sighed and looked at Mr. Adams. "These must be the 'dreamy things' you were referring to earlier. Very well, I have given you all the chances I am going to give. I will return with a warrant, and we will talk again in a more official capacity. Your secrets will come up, Ms. Adams, no matter how hard you try to bury them – they always do," he glanced to her silent companions. Half of them continued reading their leather-bound books on the sofa, and the other half turned to face Oz directly. Piper found a small air of respect for them in that moment. She was all but consciously aware that it was a show of defiance.

"There are no secrets in the light, Mr. Nolan. Only in the darkness," she responded sadly.

He left without another word. She smiled serenely as she shut the door behind him. Almost as if he had told her that she had been vindicated. However, it sounded to Piper that whatever it was, her sister had been keeping more from them than just aloof answers on what she had been doing the past four years.

Her father however, had reached his boiling point. He fumed even more than Oz. "I need to talk to you," he grabbed Lenoir forcefully by the arm. "Now!"

Her companions were already standing, Piper wasn't sure how they could do it so quickly, but they had managed it without sight or sound. Lenoir turned to them and seemed to wave them off, dismissing her father's irate action. It was the most serious Piper had seen them react to anything that occurred through the evening. She felt fearful of them again, replacing her previous impression. She had no idea why. She figured them for harmless before, but now it looked like they wanted to rip her father's head off if the situation called for it.

Lenoir's friend Scarlett approached her then, "Don't worry, they won't do anything," she placed a hand on Piper's shoulder.

"How would you even know that?" she asked but did not wait for an answer. She trailed her family toward the kitchen in an effort to figure out what was going on once and for all.

"Why won't you let me drive you to Stanford?" her dad was asking her sister.

"I was planning on going with my friends."

"You are going to need some help, if that's where you are going at all."

"It's where I am going with my friends. I'm not lying to you."

"It all just seems a little too convenient, doesn't it?"

"How so?"

"Do you not realize what you are looking at here? A man from the agency comes in and I don't know if he's going to haul you away in handcuffs or what. You run away from home without a trace or word for a few years, you come back just as suddenly, not telling us anything and uprooting all of our lives. Now you are leaving and all you give us is a lame cock and bull story about 'being accepted to Stanford' when summer is just around the corner? Are you in trouble? If you think I can't help, you're wrong. I would do anything for you. But you have to trust me enough to let me in."

"I'm going to Stanford in the morning with my friends," she reiterated, still speaking in an even tone, but the smile no longer on her face. "We have to go."

"What? Someone is forcing you to go?"

"No. It is as you said, I have wasted enough time these past years. The time for procuring a better life is now. Better lives for all of us. I apologize if my behavior is too eccentric for you. I'm just being me."

He shook his head, "I don't know this 'you.'"

She bowed her head sadly, showing another brief glimpse of sorrow before shoving it behind the smile again. "Then I'm afraid you never did."

Vincent's face dropped. Piper opened her mouth to make a sound, but nothing came out. She had never seen her sister act this way before. She was beginning to wonder if everyone was right about her. The few times since she had been home, Lenoir defended their father to Piper whenever she would try to badmouth him. There were even a few times when she tried to have a heart-to-heart with her, she told Piper that it was their only father. Even though he was not always there, he always loved them. Wasn't that what she said? *Something along those lines.* Seeing her father's face turn red and look at Lenoir that way, it was like watching the face of someone you knew age two decades in two seconds.

His face's mood lighting moved between red, purple and gray and back again. "What do you believe Lenoir?" he asked with tears in his eyes. "Tell me the truth, no bullshit, tell me what it is you believe and what the end game is for you here?"

She gazed at him, most of the conversation around them had stopped. Even some of the less mobile relatives in the next room sauntered over to witness the exchange. For a while, Piper thought that someone had finally gotten through to her. But despite the unexpected look on her face, she calmly took a breath and explained, "I believe another world exists beyond this one. A better world," she sighed, her breath stammering. "If you can somehow find your way there– I'll be waiting." She looked upon him a moment longer, and turned to go, her companions already standing up.

"Don't leave!" he called after her.

"Lenoir, come on! Where are you going?" their eldest cousin, Marie, asked.

"It's time to pray," she looked almost pained, almost broken as her companions led her away. As if they too could sense her fragile state, and only looked to comfort her in the clashing of her two worlds. Piper didn't realize it until she felt the tear roll down her cheek like some kind of frenzied waterslide, but despite her earlier thought, there was no one left to tell at this point. There was no saving her this time. No amount of interference she could give would snap her out of it. She'd watched everyone give their best effort in the few months since she had been back, but her sister was going to have to make her own choice.

The thought of it made her all the more lonely. Wishing the knock at the door had been about her troubles and not her sister's. She retreated to her room again. As everyone stood around, gawking, she heard her father say in a gruff voice that was meant to mask his sorrow, "Show's over, folks. Get out."

Later on, after everyone had left, she heard a clamor downstairs, and after some more faint rustling, a soft knock at her door. There she was in the doorway, looking pale and small; words Piper never would have used to describe her sister before.

"What do you want?" Piper asked.

"To say I'm sorry."

"I'm not sure why you're apologizing to me, you hurt dad!" Piper had been practicing what she would say if she were to get another chance with her sister. Now that the moment was here, everything she had rehearsed sounded lame out loud. "You know," she added, "'the only father we will ever have.'"

"I hurt everyone. Please forgive me for that, and for what else I have to do."

Piper glared at her, sick of her mysteries and riddles.

"Can I come in?"

"It's a free country," Piper turned back to her computer screen. She had been working feverishly on a new sketch of Mr. Unremembered ever since the party ended abruptly. This time she chose a sickly green color for him.

[211]

Lenoir joined her at the computer, she pushed a plastic package into Piper's eyesight, vying for her attention. "Here, take this."

Piper glanced down at the package; it was a cell phone. The kind you have to reload with minutes as you buy them. She gave her sister no reaction.

"My friends got it for me, but I don't need it where I'm going," she explained.

"Keep it, I have one already. Besides, you will need it at 'Stanford' once you realize everyone else has one."

"I know I hurt you too. I promise, soon your lives will be back to normal, and my intrusion will just be a dream."

"Everyone thinks you're in a cult you know," Piper stated matter-of-factly without looking up from Mr. Unremembered's new orange tie.

"It's an ugly word, but a word people use to describe ways of thinking they haven't developed yet."

Piper scoffed, "You're unbelievable. Whatever, how long do you think you will be gone this time? Five years? Ten? You going to show up at *my* high school graduation party next time?"

Lenoir only shook her head, trying her hardest to keep her composure, but looking so very broken due to the effort.

Piper looked at her again, this time it was her sister that scared her more than her companions. "How long?"

"I won't be coming back," Lenoir announced in her artificial voice.

Piper stood to leave.

"Please let me say goodbye."

"Goodbye," Piper sobbed and ran. She ran all the way out the house, down the street and to the corner. She didn't know if she would run clear out of the city, out into the desert, or if she just might make a B-line and walk straight into the ocean. Any option would have been better

[212]

than to listen to her sister's sanctimonious utterances. One thing she knew for certain was that she could not go home again. Not as long as this stranger was in their house.

Part 9
Crude Sunlight

So where are you?

You wake up with an ache in your head that feels like it may split you in half. The old familiar mantra comes advancing back to you as you gather your bearings. All the incidents of the previous evening resurface in a flood of mixed emotions.

You feel. Something you should not be able to do any longer. Wanting to shed this side effect of your humanity, you take a sweet breath of the air that nourished you for your first eighteen years. You didn't know it at the time, but those years were preparing you for exactly what you will accomplish today, as have the past few months.

You look toward the Southeast, toward Daw aba-de-le-a, you kneel, and you pray – just the way you have done countless times before. You ask for forgiveness for all your past transgressions and for guidance in your next. You thank the light for all that it has given to you, and you thank it (in vain) for the honor of meeting Isik (the true light), the being that brought everything into focus. You can feel him near, and the prospect sends you soaring to new heights. What you wouldn't give for one last communication, one last encounter, one last—

No! *You will not disgrace the light this day.*

You have come so far, yet the last offerings of your humanity linger, just like they said they would. Even more were present the previous evening. Having everyone from the past in the same place somehow made it easier, if not more motivating. Only one regret of your previous life remains, the one that led to some words of indictment against the man who raised you. While he may not belong to the light, he gave you better guidance than that. His forbidding you to leave came from a place of warmth and love, even if the light is not in his heart. Although your destiny cannot be changed, you could have placated him for a bit longer – that too would have come from a place called love, would it not? Even though the future is set; the details that involve it are fluid -- they can bend and flex with the light. You could have given him that victory. It would have made the words that followed wound less prudently. *Time to fly away now.*

As you gather your belongings: your book of the light, your wòrbdechanm, and a dozen Merkabas (the flower of the light) to bring with, you take one last aching breath. You look back on your homecoming not with regret, but with a sense of accomplishment that you passed the final test to elevate yourself to everlasting. How many could have done that under the same set of circumstances? You recall a passage much recited from your youth, 'What was, can never be, what is, is never done, and what will be, has only just begun.' It was a quote you liked enough to create that piece in your visual arts course, but you were never able to *truly* penetrate its meaning – until you were brought to the light.

Outside, with your roll of belongings under your arm, you look upon your old neighborhood with reverence. How bright it used to seem. Now that your eyes have adjusted, it looks like an alien world. As if your legs never climbed the fence along the perimeter of the garden, and your arms never breached the kitchen window when your sister locked you out. As you try to keep your sibling from your mind, you notice the neighborhood cast in shadow now. Not just because of the forthcoming dawn, but of the ugly adaptations it has settled for since you've been away.

The whole world is cast in shadow now, so much less beautiful than it was.

As expected, the rented vehicle sat idling nearby. You dimly make out Wafai's face in the driver's seat. He coaxes you in and you walk toward it with your head held high, lamenting to yourself that you will not look back. That you cannot afford to look back. You greet Wafai, Aja, Akim and the others with a familiar greeting, *Argi Luce* (Blessed light).

Argi Luce, they answer back in tandem.

They look so small dressed in their wòrbdechanm under the dingy yellow light. The van was what was foretold to you: three rows of seats removed (for no member of the light shall be seated elevated above any other member (the exception being the driver)), no windows and the color of purity. In addition to their smallness, your contemporaries also looked scared– for themselves, for you, for the rest of the world– you aren't able to say. Perhaps their trains of thought were running as swiftly as yours on this early morning.

Wafai waits as you all take a moment of silence for the fallen, the ones that had already been, and the ones yet to fall. The moment comes and passes, and still Wafai has not put the vehicle in gear. No one says anything, and immediately your mind snaps back to the principles put forth by the book of light. You see Wafai's eyes in the rearview mirror; they appear to be shuddering in anticipation. His impending destiny eclipses yours; they all do.

With barely a sound above a whisper, you recite your favorite passage from the light, the book of Isik, *We decree you will do as the light asks of you. Be strong and bold, you will not be afraid of-- nor fear the night, for the light is going with you, as you have already been unified.*

Wafai closes his eyes and does not open them back up until he puts the van in gear and pulls out rapidly into the approaching dawn. As the shadows of the budding rosewoods and Catalina cherry's grow longer until they'll be stretched out into the oblivion of daylight, you stare forward through the windscreen. You stare out at the city of Angels. The predefined roadways already grow more crowded as Monday morning approaches.

You almost suggest to Wafai to turn on the radio for one last reminder, but instead you absorb the cruel silence and shut your eyes to imagine Svarga kē rājya and how beautiful it will be when you get there. You keep reminders of the past out, and instead focus on the plans for the future. You wonder how you were able to hold on this long. You wonder whether you even had a choice. The light has the ultimate plan, and your choice is to simply bend. Even if its whims involved not one, but two failed deliveries, one passport issue at the border, and this Oz fellow, however minor his obstruction turned out to be– you bend.

You hear familiar sounds of progressive urban life as it passes you by outside, but you cannot bring yourself to look. There is nothing for you here now, in fact, there may never have been. All the wisdom you ever needed is impending, all the love you ever asked for has been given, all they need from you now is to be there. Even as Hamjin and the others in the back of the van prepare the device, you keep your eyes closed. After all, it may be the last time you are able to focus on such darkness. The clicks and clacks of the preparation marry musically to the engines and squealing brakes outside, you drift into a meditation of lusciousness before the lurching of the van slows upon meeting an earthlier terrain.

With a shudder, the rented transport rests comfortable under the hillside. You open your eyes and the blue, smoggy skies of the morning greet you. Overhead your vehicle, the great expanse of modern engineering stretches out to that blue sky. More concrete pathways leading to the heart of the city spill out from the bridge in all directions, daring to elevate themselves higher so more pathways can be constructed below. As if they could ever contend with the height the light has taken you. Motors grumble ahead at slower and slower paces as the paths fill with the unenlightened.

Ignoring them, you step out of the van as everyone tenses. Your legs and feet feel loaded with the weight you have carried with you for far too long. How wonderful it will feel to finally shed it forever. You peer around at the din of rush hour, trying your best to keep it from your mind.

There is nothing here.

Nothing besides this dense, grassy knoll beside the interstate on a Monday morning. It is a soupy, early summer sunrise. A hint of pink light shines dimly on the horizon. Before you know it, you are lying on wet, dew-stained grass.

Everything you used to do– lying down like that– *could* still be conquered, but now there is no reason. As the clouds part in and out, you could still count them. You could still gaze up longingly at the city, knowing now that it has nothing to offer you. You often used to wonder about this world, but not today. Today, there is business to attend.

But in a way, you still can't help but wonder. You look up at the bridge, and wonder about every fifth car that passes, about who they are, what they ate for breakfast, where they're going, if perhaps, doubtfully, but perhaps you knew them from some other time.

No!

They told you to never observe on a personal level. It's dangerous. Because once those stirrings relocate and shift within your heart, you become human again. And this is simply a job no human can do.

Abruptly you stand again to greet the others who have exited the vehicle along with Wafai and Aja. As time and prayer eclipse your group and the sun stretches higher, the other utility van, a twin to your own, approaches your chosen site, the underpass of the I-10 bridge that leads into downtown Los Angeles. Orion drives the other van, the others crouched similarly behind him in the cargo hold.

Underneath you are a ball of explosive energy, exhausted from travelling between your disparate worlds. No more– today you are ready for the task you've been assigned. Your numbers encroach from the other van, and you are twenty strong, just as Isik told you you would be.

As the others gather round, you greet them with the familiar *Argi Luce*, and the unfamiliar, embracing each of them as they join the larger group. Your mind turns to the light's prayer. You have rehearsed this moment a dozen times, but now that it is here, something seems off, something forces back the power of all that you hold. You take in the nineteen other faces that look longingly toward your light, awaiting your instructions. Some of them you recognize from on your way back from Maakan. Others, from the sister sanctuary in Phoenix. All have been chosen by Isik, for you. They are here to help you, to guide you, to be there when the time comes.

"Let us gather and implore," you tell them. You recite more passages from the book of Isik, words he carefully crafted over the months you helped him prepare them. You speak them now, but you can only focus on him. On beautiful, gifted, brilliant Isik. If only he could be here with you.

No!

It is not about what *you* want, it is about what is right for the light.

Still, you can't help but wonder...

The first time you met him was both frightening and blissful. You were in the darkest place you had ever been and were contemplating embracing that darkness forever.

The trip had begun well enough. Europe had been as amazing as you thought it might be, but it was not until you reached the Eastern front that you saw a hint of what your future could hold. After leaving behind the married couple you met in Greece, you arrived in Turkey on a short visa. You traveled to Gaziantep to taste Ottoman cuisine. You had never made so many wonderful connections, heard so many different viewpoints, and become so enlightened to a place outside your primitive realm. At the end of your legal expiration in Turkey, you met a man in a mosque you visited near the university. He told you of *the place* just across the border, he knew what you were and what you sought, and like the philanthropic he was, he helped arrange your passage to Aleppo.

At first, you balked at the idea of breaking such sacred, official laws in a foreign land, countering you could apply for the proper documents.

"I'm afraid they would never grant you documentation to travel there," he spoke sullenly in his broken English.

"Have I committed some crime against the people of Syria?" you mocked.

"They will see you as American, and only American, and that is as great a crime as they would allow you to commit."

You debated more of his points, but eventually relented when he described to you the wonder of travelling off grid and how much there was to see in this part of the world– a world more ancient and alive than anything you had ever seen before. After more conversation over pours of Rakı, you agreed to meet him the next morning.

He got you across the border as promised, leaving you at the edge of Aleppo in the small, holy city of Balleramoun. Amazed by its size and the friendliness of the locals you took it all in and walked over ten kilometers on sore, sandy feet. Many watched you walk down their streets in wonder, never having seen an American before. A kindly woman offered you a headdress, a custom she seemed to indicate would cause you less trouble if you partook.

But not everyone in Balleramoun was friendly. When the sky drew dark and you continued your travels East into Aleppo, you stopped at a public park to absorb the ornamentation surrounding it. As you did, you lost your bearings and wandered into an unfamiliar area. As you circled the neighborhood, you noticed a man in tattered rags following you, grunting, struggling to keep up as you tried to move faster away from him. When you tried to lose him down a narrow alley between main thoroughfares, you became trapped when you reached a locked gate.

He beat you, robbed you and cursed the Turkish lira you contained on your person, spitting at you as you lay in a ball in the corner of a cobblestoned alley. He looked for a brick, presumably to finish you off, and as he became distracted with pulling it loose, you swept his leg and ran. This was the lowest you had ever felt. Lower than when the couple in Greece attempted to ply you into joining their marriage, lower than when the pickpocket in Italy got away with your last few Italian lira-- even lower than the first time you phoned home and your father hung up on you.

This was a point Isik later identified as the universe forcing entry through the door that unlocked your soul. The man ended up with your passport, and all but ten Turkish lira, which other locals seemed to despise as much as your assailant when you attempted trade.

You wandered the next few days in a fog, starving, feeling sorry for yourself. Only able to obtain a small amount of water that you suspected contained bacteria in which you were not immune. The next step was to die in a gutter or find a U.S. consulate. You thought that a city the size of Aleppo must have one. And that became your new plan. Find someone who spoke English and could connect you with your homeland. However, no such opportunity arose. You could have called home and took back what you said to your father. He could have wired you money for a plane ticket of course, but then you never would have found the light.

How close you came to never fulfilling your true nature. How empty your life would have been thereafter. How corrupted your soul would have been for all time. How empty the feeling would have been to see another standing here in your place, fulfilling your greatest feat while you wallowed in the insipid.

After the third blister broke underneath your foot, you stopped by a beautiful fountain in a business district that looked sleek, modern and infinitely alien. The way structures had been built on this land were unlike any you had ever seen. Like you were walking down a street in someone else's dream. A someone who lay their head down on a pillow far away.

While fighting the urge to wash your horribly twisted feet in the fountain's sacred basin, you spotted a few fellows conversing with the locals. They were out of place there. They wore long white robes and spoke awkward Nafaq at best. One of them looked Anglo, albeit with a recent tone of burn from the intense sun overhead. He held a leaflet and attempted to hand it to a woman that kept her head down and tried to move around him. Twice he tried grabbing her hand, and then her walking companion became enraged, speaking five times as fast as the tanned foreigner and flapping his arms in a frenzy, pointing and making threatening gestures. The foreigner backed off and joined a group of others in similar dress. The local man continued to berate him in Nafaq, walking backwards as his presumable wife pulled him along.

You placed your sandal back on your blistered foot, trying your best to smile at the older woman scowling in your direction, and took a breath before you walked towards the group. Most looked local, but in addition to the foreigner, there was also a girl a bit older than you of Western Asian descent. She smiled and spoke with the others. As you came closer, you realized they were all speaking in Nafaq.

You cleared your throat and hobbled up to them, they stood silent and awestruck as you approached, "hal yatahadath ahd al'iinjlizia," you tried your best.

From the looks upon their faces, you did not impress them; they continued to stare, seeming unable to speak. "'aw alhulandia," you tried again. "'aw al'almania," you grew desperate. The pained look upon your face as you shifted your feet, hitting one of your blisters dead center on a pointy pebble, snapped them out of their shock.

"American?" the tanned foreigner smiled warmly.
You nodded.

"Hadha tariq tawil min almanzil," he mentioned to the others. They nodded in agreement, but also, they smiled at you, filling you with the most beautiful kind of hope you ever felt. You were only thinking of your desires at the time, but how could you not know at that moment what greatness was in store for you?

Later, long after they brought you to Maakan, to the light -- onward to the path that led you here, Isik told you they felt your aura as soon as you spoke. That was why they stared at you like that.

"I figured it was my shabby appearance," you confided.

"Those who follow the light, do not care for exteriors. However, your beauty matches your spirit and your significance," he paused, touching your face. You later came to yearn for that touch all the time. When Isik touched you, it felt like the whole world stopped what it was doing, turned toward you, and thanked you for all you have done for it. Like being called a hero for something that came naturally over and over again to the point of embarrassment. Like someone had just given you the most thoughtful gift, something you didn't expect, and never would have dreamed of on your own, but brought you a peace that you didn't even know you needed.

It was the next day the foreigner, a German man who called himself Himmlisch, brought you to *the place*. The only temple that was built to hold the true source of the light. A place where understanding and fulfillment of spirit reached its potential. It was unlike anything you had seen before. You should have been afraid, but an inexorable pull drew you toward the heart of the temple. A need to know.

You stepped inside and they welcomed you, all of it was born from a wonderful dream. The rest of the world seemed so ugly compared to how the temple lived. However, it was not the aesthetic in *the place* that beckoned you, nor was it the warm, friendly welcomes, it was the promise of true understanding. To look at yourself in the mirror and truly know if existence was real or if your waking life was authored by a higher, more intelligent power. In that moment, when you reached the mirror and looked, you saw yourself, surrounded by the light. You lived a thousand lifetimes filled with bliss from that viewing and would live a thousand more lifetimes of the same during your time in Makaan, with Isik.

A pain emerges on your face as you drift back from this memory. It's like pulling yourself out of a warm bath in the dead of winter. How badly you want to be back there. How inherently difficult it is to proceed with your fate when all you want to do is live those blissful lifetimes over again.

To regain your composure, you reach down to the ground, scoop up a fistful of earth and rub it in your eyes, reminding you that pain, like bliss, is only subjective and temporary. Sacrifice is much more admirable a sacrifice that will bring about the broadcasting of the light to all.

A haze in the air allows you to peer into the future. Of how beautiful your contribution will be. Of how free you and the nineteen others that surround you will be.

You are perfect. They told you so.

An American girl with hair the color of the light and the presence of an angel.

A former daddy's girl.

A rebellious teen.

A dedicated sister.

[225]

A natural born leader.

Instead of using your exteriors for useless temptation, you apply them to another cloak and dagger scheme.

You look up to the Milky Way and ache for one last drop of rain. Something to cool the burning desire you have to make the world perfect. To make it yours.

It may not come...

Looking back down at the faces of your disciples jars you from this egotistical state. Their looks are of horror and anguish, likely because they can feel the selfishness rising within you. Somewhere in the back of your mind's eye, you think they may actually be disturbed by the selfless act you had all gathered there to commit. If Isik were here now, he would tell you you were being insolent again.

How you hated to disappoint him.

How disenchanted you were with yourself on those days where you didn't fulfill your responsibilities, where your prayers were said with half a heart, where your blessings toward the light felt hollow– especially when Isik's eyes rolled back and he said, "Insolent child. Perhaps your impudence disguised itself as light."

After you swore to him that it hadn't, and that your momentary lapse had vacated for good, he feigned indifference. To impress him, you expressed your opinion on a passage you had read in his previous book *The Burning of the Light's Mind* in which a cynic of the light could have the darkness torn out of them.

The light heals all wounds, you recited his words back to him, *even the wounds the light smotes upon the skeptic to make one's will strong, and spirit more powerful towards the light, rather than against it.*

You begged him to save you in the way described. To tear the darkness out of you.

He performed the ceremony at midnight. It took you weeks to recover from your wounds, but it worked. That was the day you lay down your arms to the light– to him– to your old self. That was the day Lenoir ceased to exist.

You are determined not to make that day a mistake.

"Let us lift our heads up toward the light," you begin. They mimicked your stance, sitting crossed legged with your hands held up toward the towering bridge. "Bless this structure as the portal it is in which the light will emerge from its holy temple. While the light is always with us and need not be summoned, it has, in its everlasting wisdom and mercy decided to show itself today, by channeling our spirits. Today we lift ourselves up to the light, we can shed our mortal weaknesses to give ourselves over fully to its teachings. Thank you, Isik, for showing us the path toward everlasting, thank you for the security and warmth you have given us in this world as you prepare to send us to the superior one. Thank you for taking our burdens, laying them at your feet and allowing us passage to the light with clean spirits. We thank you for this opportunity, this chance to craft the world we all want. Thank you for your presence here today and in the eternal."

The sky smog is clearing, eight A.M. is fast approaching. Horns and friction loaded rubber moving across an artificial yellow brick road becomes more frequent. You have watched them move aimlessly the last few weeks, from this spot– your final bout of preparation. Always at this time, and then back again in the opposite direction a third of a day later. On the start of the weekends, you watched them too. You watched them drive like dark fiends toward their destinations. You watched them move further out of the light's reach toward their cottage in the country, their oasis in the desert, their penthouse in the financial district, their cabin in the woods, their circus in heaven and their igneous in hell.

Like a sociologist that picked a site to study over the long term, you always hoped for a different result each day you observed. You always hoped this gloomy place that birthed you would change its course and find the light all on its own. Much the way a parent to a troubled child hopes they can turn their life around before it's too late. Or the way those who hope to find peace continue to pray even as their worlds crumble around them. Prayer and meditation are cornerstones of hope. Hope never dies, but sometimes it is not enough.

No matter.

Soon, they will all awake for the first time. They'll see what you and the rest see. You'll see what they see.

You ignore the others around you and picture it in your mind's eye. You peer through the hazy discord that has knotted within you, and you can see the future again. You have witnessed first-hand what the hand of the light– the yd alqadr– can do to this world. You witnessed firsthand the bombing in Amman. You saw roofs ripped from buildings, the trees and shrubs snapped like toothpicks. You heard the cries of pain from the mothers, the fathers– the guttural bellowings of those pierced with twenty pieces of shrapnel, sometimes more. Here could be the same.

When the fire of the light is ignited, the force of it will build incredible pressure from within – like shaking up a can of soda pop. When that pressure can no longer be contained, the hull of this society will break, and the fire will stream upward. It won't be fire at first, it will be a wall of invisible energy. It will slam against the deck of the bridge with limitless power, crumbling blocks of concrete as thick as train cars. The flanges and studs will buckle, causing the deck to fold and crumble. Their self-inflicted metal cages will tumble down one after the other. As that is happening, gravity will pull the fire back toward earth and scorch it where you sit. Judging by the Santa Ana winds blowing today and the lack of precipitation lately, an inferno could spread across the small inlet where you parked your vans. When the deck of the bridge crumbles completely, it may take the surrounding ones with it, or the steel skeleton within may hold on enough to keep them dangling. By then, the dust and debris, lighter than any of the cars or other material, will be swirling and pluming up, rising to meet the light.

The twisted metal will bind together under the force of crumbling concrete and searing heat, and by that time, the burning fuel, the arid fauna and the earth shaken to its core will spread across the land. What will they find then? They will find that you turned their skins inside out so that this world can see the ugliness of its insides. What will they find after the dust settles? They will find a sea of their growing atrocities all warped together like a work of art, then they will begin to understand the blind spots they had been peering through. The false idols they have been following. The charlatans they have become. They'll look at the blackened blanket of ash over the soil and realize it is not permanent— no— a new and better world will take its place. More soldiers fighting for the light will take yours.

When the smoke finally clears and the sirens cease, they will repent you in infamy. Not as another Barbie doll in a sea of bleached telecommunications, but a pioneer in the thick of change, a history that has yet to be molded, still waiting to dry and take shape.

You open your eyes back up and take the hand of the being next to you, Drago. You remember seeing him in a temple in Malaan. He is frightened to his very core. His hands shake uncontrollably and his garment sticks to his back from sweat. "When it's time," you say to him, "I'll be right here."

He nods exhaustively, but he doesn't take his eyes off you. He is absolutely enamored with your sacrifice, more than even his own.

We all are.

You pluck a few Merkabas from your roll of belongings and hand them out to the enlightened. A final offering of encouragement from Isik. Then you nod to Wafai, "It is time."

He hands you the device with a mixture of determination and wonderment on his face. You thank him as you cradle it in your arms, breaking hands from the circle for a moment. You see the place around you evolve over a short period of time. You see the blackness that will soon embark, and the birth of the enlightened world from the ashes that wilt away. From your ashes comes a new light.

And that is the pinnacle of your being. No person has ever understood their place in the world as you have. So, it's only right to give the greatest gift you have back to it.

Your understanding is exposed to the others, and they seem to take a kind of relief from it.

You sigh the deepest breath you can muster and slowly caress the rainbow circuitry of the device. They almost feel like the nimble fingers of a far-off lover. Someone you never meant to hurt but got too close.

A cry escapes Drago next to you. His inner darkness is showing, perhaps he has unfinished business in this place. Perhaps his homecoming was not as bright as he hoped it would be. Perhaps he tried so hard to bring those from his previous life to the light but failed anyway. His attempts were not in vain. Which is why you can only assure him by placing your hands over him and shutting your eyes real tight. "Together our strength, together our wake. Together to the Kingdom," you tell him.

You always knew you were meant for more than being another link in a futile, proverbial chain.

He nods again, and you all look upon one another once more.

You always knew great things were in store for you.

So, you take in the sweetest, clearest, cleanest breath the earth has to offer this morning, retake the hand of the being next to you, and firmly press down on molded plastic.

You always knew you would change the world.

[230]

It soon sends charges of ions through you. From plastic to plastique. A deafening light and a blinding scream.

You knew because they told you. They believed in you. *He* believed in you.

A ruby red smile comes to the last of your face. A sensation warmer than blood, but cooler than wind.

A homecoming more satisfying than any piece of art, flesh or alternate state could possibly provide.

--I'm still waiting for you; tell me I did good. Tell me I did right by the light.

So where are you?

--Tell me you love me, Isik.

You're home.

--Tell me.

This book was begun on July 30th, 2015 and finished December 7th 2019. Final editing was completed on July 19th, 2021. Proof was finished at the end of 2023.

Acknowledgements:

This book is dedicated to those who have lost family, friends or significant others to the influence of religion, cults, etc. This includes the countless wars declared in the name of God. It's for anyone who was a victim of others who couldn't stand to look truth in the eye. There is no control, power or order. There is only us.

This book is also dedicated to those who have lost connections to those they were once close. The loss of relationships and our ability to save them is the real-life villain of our society. We must not allow our differing beliefs, customs, and values poison them further.

Finally, a special acknowledgement must be paid to those who have suffered from extremist actions or terrorism. Following ideals only hurts you, inflicting them on others hurts everyone.

Thanks to Debby Frost for the amazing cover art. Thank you for entertaining all my nuisance suggestions and for humoring me with excitement and energy.

Thanks to all who read it first, gave me notes, and ultimately, the courage to self-publish again. This book is for you.

Special thanks to my wife, Carrie (my true light) for seeing me through my own darkness and meeting me on the other side.

Finally, thanks to all that lead the fight in protecting our books, words, knowledge and information. More importantly, fighting to protect our access to them. You are the true saints, walis and Tzaddics.

Note on the Font:

The main prose of this book uses the Garamond typeface, original designed by Claude Garamond in the 16th century. The typeface was originally used in the printing of books in Roman and Latin. Later iterations of the typeface boast specific designs used by large companies such as the original Google logo, and Adobe.

The communications to Lenoir use the Calibri font. A digital sans-serif typeface designed by Microsoft to become the default font and to replace Times New Roman. In typography terms, Calibri is designated as a Humanist font, which couldn't be more appropriate for this story.

For more information on titles by Christian Hendrix, including notes, documents, and other content for "You Can't Go Home Again," please visit his website:

www.christian-hendrix.com

Christian Hendrix is the author of five novels, many short stories and three almost-novel-length novellas. He is a librarian, a video gamer, a novice piano player, digital data hoarder, endless reddit scroller, news junkie, a concert and cinema attendee, and many other multipotentialite activities. Christian considers himself a hedonistic generalist that is interested in many activities without mastering any of them. When he's not reading or writing, he is known to blast Trance music and go on long bike rides. He lives with his wife and dog incognito in an expansive, nondescript suburb outside of St. Paul, MN.